Colin turned sharply on his heel and glared at this woman who wouldn't take a hint.

"Lady—"

"Miranda," she prompted.

"Miranda," Colin echoed between gritted teeth. "You are a royal pain, you know that?"

Miranda always tried to glean something positive out of every situation, no matter how bleak it might appear. "Does that mean you'll look for her?" she asked him hopefully.

He blew out an angry breath. "That means you're a royal pain," he repeated.

With nothing to lose, Miranda went out on a limb. "Please? I can give you a description of Lily's mother." And then she thought of something even better. "And if you come with me, I can get you a picture of her that'll be useful."

He had a feeling that the woman just wasn't going to give up unless he agreed to help her. Although it irritated him beyond description, there was a very small part of him that did admire her tenacity.

* * *

MATCHMAKING MAMAS:
Playing Cupid. Arranging dates.
What are mothers for?

Dear Reader,

You know how sometimes you get a song stuck in your head that you just can't get rid of? Well, in my case that doesn't just happen with songs. Sometimes it's a phrase, but more often, it's a title. Case in point, years ago my first Romantic Suspense was entitled *Holding Out for a Hero*. That song was part of the score for a movie my kids loved enough that I took them to it several times. It was a cute movie, but I couldn't get that song out of my head for weeks. I carried that title around for a number of years until I came up with a story that warranted it.

I had the same thing happen a number of years after that with a title that popped into my head and refused to "unpop." The title this time was *Good Deeds and Miranda*. This time, sadly, my choice for a title was vetoed, but that doesn't change the fact that this book was born to tell that title's story.

Miranda Steele is a perpetual do-gooder. The die was cast when Miranda's sister, Emily, died of leukemia at the age of five. Miranda loved her and saw herself as her sister's protector. She refocused all her energy to helping others, be they children, adults or animals. She has so many outlets for her good deeds that she doesn't have any time for herself—until loner Colin Kirby crosses her path. The police officer has witnessed too much death for his young age, and the only way he's found to survive is to withdraw into himself. When their paths cross (by arrangement, thanks to the Matchmaking Mamas), Miranda sees a broken soul who needs comfort and a way to get back among the living. Colin sees an attractive whirling dervish who just won't leave him alone—until he doesn't want to be left alone.

As always, thank you for taking the time to read my book, and from the bottom of my heart, I wish you someone to love who loves you back.

All the best,

Marie

Christmastime Courtship

Marie Ferrarella

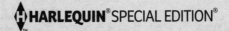

HARLEQUIN® SPECIAL EDITION®

Recycling programs
for this product may
not exist in your area.

ISBN-13: 978-0-373-62389-1

Christmastime Courtship

Printed in U.S.A.

USA TODAY bestselling and RITA® Award—winning author **Marie Ferrarella** has written more than two hundred and seventy-five books for Harlequin, some under the name Marie Nicole. Her romances are beloved by fans worldwide. Visit her website, marieferrarella.com.

Books by Marie Ferrarella

Harlequin Special Edition

Matchmaking Mamas

A Second Chance for the Single Dad
Meant to Be Mine
Twice a Hero, Always Her Man
Dr. Forget-Me-Not
Coming Home for Christmas
Her Red-Carpet Romance
Diamond in the Ruff
Dating for Two
Wish Upon a Matchmaker
Ten Years Later...
A Perfectly Imperfect Match
Once Upon a Matchmaker

The Montana Mavericks: The Great Family Roundup
The Maverick's Return

The Fortunes of Texas: The Secret Fortunes
Fortune's Second-Chance Cowboy

Montana Mavericks: The Baby Bonanza
A Maverick and a Half

Montana Mavericks: What Happened at the Wedding?
Do You Take This Maverick?

The Fortunes of Texas: Cowboy Country
Mendoza's Secret Fortune

Visit the Author Profile page
at Harlequin.com for more titles.

To
Melany,
The Best Daughter-in-Law
Anyone Could Ask For.
Welcome To The Family.

Prologue

"Is it true?"

Theresa Manetti looked up from the menu she was putting the final touches on to see who had just walked into her inner office. Most clients who wanted to avail themselves of her catering services either called or were brought in by one of her staff and announced.

As it turned out, this time Theresa found herself looking up at Jeannine Steele, an old friend she hadn't seen in at least six months. Not since she'd catered Jeannine's husband's funeral reception.

"Well, that's a new kind of greeting," Theresa commented, amused. "Most people usually say hello. Is *what* true?" she asked, nodding toward the chair on the other side of her desk, indicating that her friend should sit down.

Looking uncomfortable and nervous, Jeannine

lowered herself onto the chair, perching on its edge. "There's a rumor going around that in addition to your catering business, you're running some sort of a dating service on the side."

Theresa had known Jeannine since her own two children had been in elementary school with Jeannine's daughter, and in all that time, she couldn't recall the stately woman appearing anything but completely in control.

Always.

But not this time.

"Well, that's not exactly an accurate description," Theresa replied. "It's not really a 'dating service,' so much as a matchmaking service."

Confusion furrowed Jeannie's otherwise smooth, alabaster brow. "There's a difference?"

From her vantage point, Theresa could see the other woman twisting her long, slender fingers together. Theresa was experienced enough to know where this was heading, and did what she could to set her friend at ease.

"A big difference," she answered, pushing back her chair and rising to her feet. "Would you like something to drink, Jeannine?" she asked kindly. "I have everything from tea to soft drinks to something a little more 'bracing' if you'd rather have that."

Jeannine drew in a deep breath before answering. "I'll take tea," she replied. "Strong tea."

Theresa smiled as she went to the counter against the back wall, where she had a pot of hot water steaming. She had a preference for tea herself.

"So, it's been a while, Jeannine," she said in her customary easygoing manner. "How are you?"

"Concerned, frankly," the other woman admitted.

Recrossing the room, Theresa held out the cup of tea. "You're worried about Miranda, aren't you?"

Her friend nearly dropped the cup Theresa had handed her. Some hot liquid sloshed over the side. "How did you know?" she asked, surprised.

"To begin with, you asked me about my so-called 'sideline,'" Theresa answered, employing a whimsical term for the labor that had become near and dear not just to her heart, but to Maizie's and Celia's hearts, as well.

Theresa and the two women she had been best friends with since the third grade had weathered all of life's highs and lows together. The highs included marriage, children and the successful businesses all three had started in the second half of their lives and were currently running.

The lows included all three becoming widows. But she, Maizie and Celia had learned to push on past the pain. After all, they each had children to provide for. They were determined to lead productive, fulfilling lives. And above all else, they were always, always there for one another.

Their matchmaking had begun slowly, by finding matches for their own children. That was to be the end of it, but matching up the right two people brought such satisfaction with it, they'd decided to try their hand at it again.

And again.

With each successful match, their secondary vocation just seemed to take wings. They loved the businesses they had begun and nurtured individually, but there was something exceedingly fulfilling about bringing together two people who otherwise might never have found one another.

Two people who clearly belonged together.

It looked as if the adventure was about to begin again, Theresa thought.

"Tell me about Miranda," she coaxed, taking her seat once more. "How is she? Is she still as wonderfully generous and big-hearted as ever?"

Jeannine thought of her only daughter—her only living child—whose career path had been chosen at the age of ten. "Yes—and that's the problem. She's so busy giving of herself, working at the children's hospital, the women's shelter *and* the city's animal shelter, that she doesn't have any time to focus on herself. Don't get me wrong, Theresa. I'm prouder of Miranda than I can possibly say, but, well, I'm really afraid that if she keeps going like this, she's eventually going to wind up alone." Jeannine sighed. "I know that sounds like I'm being small-minded and meddling, but—"

Theresa cut her short. "Trust me, I know the feeling," she assured her. "We're mothers, Jeannine. It comes with the territory." With her business going full steam ahead the way it was these days, she could use a little diversion. "Tell me, do you have any idea what Miranda's dating life is like?"

"I have a very clear idea," Jeannine replied. "It's nonexistent these days."

"Really?"

"Really," she confirmed sadly. "The problem is that no man can compete with her full-time job, as well as all her volunteer work. Besides, what man wants to come in fourth?"

"Definitely not the kind of man we would want for your daughter," Theresa said with conviction.

Jeannine looked confused. "What are you saying?"

Theresa smiled as she began making plans. "I'm saying we need to change Miranda's focus a little."

"So you do think there's hope?" A glimmer of optimism entered the other woman's hazel eyes.

Theresa leaned over and patted her friend's hand. "Jeannine," she said confidently, "there is *always* hope."

Chapter One

"Ladies, we have work to do," Theresa announced the moment she entered Maizie Sommer's house.

She strode into Maizie's family room with the vigor of a woman half her age. Matchmaking projects always got her adrenaline going, creating a level of enthusiasm within her even greater than her usual line of work did—and it went without saying that she dearly loved her catering business.

"We certainly do," Cecilia Parnell agreed.

Already seated at the card table—their usual gathering place whenever they were discussing their newest undertaking in the matchmaking arena—Celia turned to look at her. "This one is going to be a real challenge for us."

"Oh, I don't know," Theresa protested, gracefully slipping into the chair that was set up between Celia and Maizie. "I don't think it'll be *that* hard finding someone suitable."

Taken aback, Celia looked quizzically at her old friend, who hadn't called ahead with any details about the person she felt should be their latest project. "Wait, how would you know?"

"How would I know?" Theresa repeated incredulously. "Because I've known Miranda Steele ever since she was a little girl. She has this incredibly huge heart and she's always trying to help everyone. Fix everyone," Theresa emphasized, which was why she had come to think of the young woman as "the fixer" in recent years.

"Miranda?" Celia echoed, decidedly more confused than she'd initially been. "Maizie and I were talking about Colin when you walked in."

It was Theresa's turn to be confused. "Who's Colin?" she asked, looking from Maizie to Celia.

"Police Officer Colin Kirby," Celia clarified, adding, "our latest matchmaking project. His aunt Lily is a friend of mine and she came to talk to me on the outside chance that maybe I—actually *we*—could find someone for him."

Without pausing, Celia launched into a brief version of the police officer's backstory. "Lily took him in when her sister, Vanessa, a single mother, died in a car accident. Colin was fourteen at the time. She said that he's a decent, hardworking young man who just shut down when he lost his mother. He enlisted in the Marines straight out of high school. When his tour of duty overseas ended, he was honorably discharged and immediately joined the police force in Los Angeles."

Maizie appeared a little dubious. "Los Angeles is a little out of our usual territory," she commented. "But I guess—"

"Oh no." Celia quickly cut in. "He's not in Los Angeles anymore, he's in Bedford now. Lily talked him into moving back down here. Her health isn't what it used to be and he's her only living relative, so he made the move for her, which, in my book, shows you what sort of a person he is.

"The problem is," Celia continued, "Lily says he's really closed off, especially after what he saw during his tour overseas and as a police officer in one of the roughest areas in Los Angeles. To put it in Lily's own words," she concluded, "Colin needs someone to 'fix him.'"

Smiling, Maizie shifted her gaze from Celia to Theresa. It was obvious that, in her estimation, they needed to look no further in either case. "You just said you have someone who likes to 'fix' people."

But Celia was more skeptical than her friend. She needed more to work with. "Fix how?"

Theresa gave them Miranda's background in a nutshell. "According to her mother, Miranda's a pediatric nurse at Bedford Children's Hospital who volunteers at a women's shelter in her free time. She also volunteers at the city's animal shelter and occasionally takes in strays until they can be placed in a permanent home."

Maizie's smile widened. "Ladies, maybe I'm getting ahead of myself, but this sounds to me like a match made in heaven. I'm assuming you both have a few more pertinent details that we can work with—like what these two look like and how old they are, for openers," said the woman whose decision to find her daughter a suitable match had initially gotten what turned out to be their "side business" rolling eight years ago.

"Miranda's thirty," Theresa told them, producing a photograph on her smartphone that Jeannie had sent her, and holding it up for the others to see.

"Colin's thirty-three," Celia said. "And I'll ask Lily to send me a picture."

So saying, she texted a message to the woman. In less than a minute, her cell phone buzzed, announcing that her request had been received and answered.

"Here we go," Celia declared. "Oh my," she murmured as she looked at the image that had materialized on her smartphone. Colin's aunt had sent her a photo of her nephew in his police uniform.

Maizie took Celia's hand and turned the phone around so she could look at it.

"Definitely 'oh my,'" she agreed wholeheartedly. Pushing the deck of cards aside, she gave up all pretense that they were going to engage in a game of poker this evening, even a single hand. Her gaze took in her two lifelong friends. "Ladies, let's get down to work. These two selfless servants of society need us. And from what I've heard, they also need each other," the successful Realtor added knowingly. "We'll require more information to bring about the perfect subtle 'meet' to get this particular ball rolling."

Filled with anticipation, the three old friends got busy.

Every year, the holiday season seemed to begin earlier and earlier, Miranda Steele thought.

Not that she was complaining. Christmas had always been her very favorite time of year. While others grumbled that the stores were putting up Christmas decorations way too soon, motivated by a desire to increase their already obscene profits, Miranda saw it as a way to stretch the spirit of Christmas a little further, thereby making the true meaning of the season last a little longer.

But sometimes, like now, the pace became a little too hectic even for her. She had just put in a ten-hour day at the hospital, coming in way before her shift actually began in order to help decorate the oncology ward, where she worked. She felt particularly driven because she knew that for some of the children there it would be their last Christmas.

As harsh and sad as that thought was to deal with, she chose to focus on the bright side: bringing the best possible Christmas she could to the children and their families.

At times, she felt like a lone cheerleader, tirelessly attempting to drum up enthusiasm and support from the other nurses, doctors and orderlies on the floor until she had everyone finally pitching in, even if they weren't all cheerful about it.

She didn't care if the rest of the staff was cheerful or not, as long as they helped out. And as was her habit, she worked harder than anyone to make sure that things were ultimately "just right."

If she were a normal person, about now she would be on her way home, having earned some serious bubble bath time.

But soaking in a hot tub was not on this afternoon's

agenda. She didn't have time for a bubble bath, as much as she longed for one. She had to get Lily's birthday party ready.

Lily Hayden was eight today. The little girl was one of the many children currently living with their moms at the Bedford Women's Home, a shelter where Miranda volunteered four days a week after work.

The other two or three days she spent at the city's no-kill animal shelter, where she worked with dogs and cats—and the occasional rabbit—that were rescued from a possible bleak demise on the street. Miranda had an affinity for all things homeless, be they four-footed or two-footed. In her opinion there never seemed to be enough hours in the day for her to help all these deserving creatures.

She had been working in all three areas for years now and felt she had barely been able to scratch the surface.

Agitated, Miranda looked at the clock on her dashboard. The minutes were flying by.

She was running the risk of being late.

"And if you don't get there with this cake, Lily is going to think you've forgotten all about her, just like her mom did," Miranda muttered to herself.

Lily's mother had left the little girl at the shelter when she'd gone to look for work. That was two days ago. No one had heard from the woman since. Miranda was beginning to worry that Gina Hayden, overwhelmed with her circumstances, had bailed out, using the excuse that the little girl was better off at the shelter, without her.

Stepping on the gas, Miranda made a sharp right

turn at the next corner, reaching out to hold the cake box on the passenger seat in place.

Focused on getting to the homeless shelter on time, Miranda wasn't aware of the dancing red and blue lights behind her until she heard the siren, high-pitched, demanding and shrill, slicing through the air. The sound drew her attention to the lights, simultaneously making her stomach drop with a jarring thud.

Oh damn, why today of all days? Miranda silently demanded as, resigned to her fate, she pulled her car over to the right. Even as she did so, something inside her wanted to push her foot down on the accelerator and just take off.

But considering that her newfound nemesis was riding a motorcycle and her car was a fifteen-year-old asthmatic vehicle way past its glory days, a clean getaway was simply not in the cards.

So she pulled over and waited for her inevitable ticket, fervently hoping the whole process was not going to take too long. She was already behind schedule. Miranda didn't want to disappoint Lily, who had already been disappointed far too often in her short life.

This wasn't his usual route. For some unknown reason, the desk sergeant had decided that today, he and Kaminski were going to trade routes.

Sergeant Bailey had made the switch, saying something about "mixing things up and keeping them fresh"—whatever that was supposed to mean, Colin thought, grumbling under his breath.

As far as he was concerned, one route was as good as

another. At least here in Bedford the only thing people shot at him were dirty looks, instead of bullets from the muzzles of illegally gotten handguns. He had to admit that patrolling the streets of Bedford was a far cry from patrolling the barrio in Los Angeles, or driving on the roads in Afghanistan. In those situations, a man had to develop eyes in the back of his head to stay alive.

Here in Bedford, those same eyes were in danger of shutting, but from boredom, not a fatal shot.

He supposed, after everything he had been through in the last ten years, a little boredom was welcome—at least for a while.

But he didn't exactly like the idea of hiding on the far side of the underpass, waiting to issue a ticket to some unsuspecting Bedford resident.

Yet those were the rules of the game here, and for now, he wasn't about to rock the boat.

First and foremost, he was here because of Aunt Lily. Because he owed her big-time. She had taken him in when no one else would, and to his discredit, he had repaid her by shutting her out and being surly. It wasn't her fault he had behaved that way; the blame was his.

In his defense—if he could call it that—he hadn't wanted to risk forming another attachment, only to have to endure the pain that came if and when he lost her. Lost her the way he'd lost everyone else in his life that ever mattered. His mother. Some of the men in his platoon. And Owens, his last partner in LA.

Colin's method of preventing that sort of pain was to cut himself off from everyone. That way, the pain had no chance of ever taking root, no chance of slicing him off at the knees.

At least that was what he told himself.

Still, he reasoned, playing his own devil's advocate, if there wasn't some part of him that cared, that was still capable of forming some sort of an attachment, however minor, would he have uprooted himself the way he had in order to be here because Aunt Lily had asked him to?

He didn't know.

Or maybe he did, and just didn't want to admit it to himself.

Either way, it wasn't something that was going to be resolved today. Today he needed to focus on the small stuff.

Right now he had a speeder to stop, he told himself, coming to life and increasing his own speed.

Because the woman in the old sedan was obviously not looking into her rearview mirror, Colin turned on his siren.

There, that got her attention. At least she wasn't one of those foolhardy birdbrains who thought they could outrace his motorcycle, Colin observed, as the car began to decrease its speed.

Watching the vehicle slow down and then come to a stop, Colin braced himself for what he knew was about to come. Either the driver was going to turn on the waterworks, attempting to cry her way out of a ticket by appealing to what she hoped was his chivalrous nature, or she was going to be belligerent, demanding to know if he had nothing better to do than to harass otherwise law-abiding citizens by issuing speeding tickets for offenses that were hardly noteworthy, instead of pursuing real criminals.

After parking his motorcycle behind her vehicle, he got off, then took his time walking up to the offending driver. Because the street was a busy one, with three lanes going in each direction, Colin made his way to the passenger side, to avoid getting hit by any passing motorist.

As he approached, he motioned for the driver to roll down her window.

She looked nervous. Well, the woman should have thought about this before she'd started speeding.

"Do you know why I pulled you over?" he asked gruffly.

Miranda took a breath before answering. "Because I was speeding."

A little surprised at the simplicity of her reply, Colin waited for more.

It didn't come.

The woman wasn't trying to talk her way out of the ticket she obviously knew was coming. He found that rather unusual. In his experience, people he pulled over in Bedford weren't normally this calm, or this seemingly polite.

Colin remained on his guard, anticipating a sudden turn on the driver's part.

"Right," he said, picking up on her answer. "You were speeding. Any particular reason why?"

He was aware that he was giving her the perfect opportunity to attempt to play on his sympathies, with some sort of a sob story. Such as she'd just gotten a call from the hospital saying her mother or father or some other important person in her life had just had a heart attack, and she was rushing to their side before they died.

He'd heard it all before. The excuses got pretty creative sometimes.

He had to admit that, for some reason, he was mildly curious to hear what this driver had to offer as *her* excuse.

"There's this little girl at the homeless shelter. It's her birthday today and I'm bringing the cake. The party starts in ten minutes and I got off my shift at the hospital later than I anticipated. I work at Children's Hospital and we had an emergency," she explained, inserting a sidebar.

"Where at Children's Hospital?" Colin asked, wondering just how far the woman was going to take this tale she was spinning.

"The oncology ward," she answered.

He should have seen that one coming. "Really?" he challenged.

Was he asking her for proof? That was simple enough, she thought. Because she'd been in such a rush, she was still wearing her uniform, and she had her hospital badge around her neck.

Holding up her ID, she showed it to him. "Yes, really, Officer," she answered politely. "Now if you'll please write out the ticket and give it to me so I can be on my way, I can still make the party on time. I don't want Lily to think I forgot about her, today of all days."

About to begin doing so, Colin looked up sharply. "Lily?" he questioned.

"That's her name," Miranda answered. "Lily."

Colin stared at the woman, a stoic expression on his face as he tried to make up his mind if she was actually serious, or trying to con him.

She couldn't possibly know about his aunt, he decided.

"My aunt's name is Lily," he told her, watching her face for some telltale sign that she was making all this up.

"It's a nice name," Miranda responded, waiting for him to begin writing.

Colin paused for a long moment, weighing the situation.

And then he did something he didn't ordinarily do. Actually, it was something he'd *never* done before. He closed his ticket book.

"All right, I'm letting you off with a warning," he told her. Then added an ominous "Watch yourself," before he turned on his heel and walked back to his motorcycle.

Chapter Two

Miranda's first impulse was to take off before the officer decided to change his mind about writing her that ticket. But as she thought about the fact that she had just dodged a bullet, an idea came to her. Rather than start her car and drive away under the police officer's watchful eye, Miranda opened her door and got out of her beloved vehicle.

"Officer?" she called, raising her voice.

Colin had already gotten on his motorcycle. Surprised, he looked in her direction. After a beat, he sighed and then slowly dismounted.

Now what? he silently demanded.

"Something on your mind, miss?" he asked, his voice low and far from friendly.

The officer sounded as if she was annoying him. But Miranda hadn't gotten where she was by giving in to the nervous quiver that occasionally popped up in her stomach—as it did now.

Raising her head so that her eyes met his—or where she assumed his eyes were, because he'd lowered the visor on his helmet, she stated, "I wanted to say thank you."

Colin grunted in response, because in his opinion, this wasn't the sort of situation where "you're welcome" suited the occasion. As far as he was concerned, she wasn't welcome. He'd just given in to an impulse that had come out of nowhere, and if he thought about it now, he was rather bewildered by his own actions.

"Do you have a card?" she asked him.

"A card?" Colin repeated, clearly perplexed by her question.

Miranda didn't think she was asking for anything out of the ordinary. "Yes, like a business card. The police department issues those to you, right?"

Instead of answering her question, or giving her one of the cards he carried in his pocket, Colin asked, "Why do you want it? You don't have anything to report me for," he pointed out gruffly.

It took Miranda a second to absorb what he was saying. Talk about being defensive. But then, maybe he had a reason. Some people were belligerent when dealing with the police.

"I don't want to report you," she assured him with feeling. "I just want to be able to call you."

So that was it, Colin thought. The woman was a groupie. He knew that there were people—mostly women—who were attracted to the uniform, some to the point of obsession. He had no patience when it came to groupies.

Colin got back on his motorcycle, ready to take off. "That's not a good idea," he told her in a voice that left no room for argument.

Or at least he thought it didn't.

"But the kids at the hospital would get such a big kick out of meeting a real live motorcycle cop," she said, hoping to change his mind.

She caught him completely off guard. He definitely hadn't been expecting that.

Now that he had transferred to Bedford, he didn't find himself interacting with any children. The ones back in the LA neighborhood he used to patrol saw police officers as the enemy, and either scattered whenever they saw him coming, or would throw things at him and *then* run.

"Look, I don't think—" Colin got no further than that.

Determined to convince him, Miranda attempted to submerge the police officer in a tidal wave of rhetoric. "A lot of the kids in that ward haven't been out of the hospital in months. I think meeting you would go a long way in cheering them up."

There had to be some sort of an ulterior motive at work here, Colin thought, and he wasn't about to fall for whatever trap she was trying to set for him.

"I really doubt that," he told her as he revved his motorcycle.

"I don't," Miranda countered cheerfully, refusing to be put off. "Why don't you come by the hospital and we'll see which one of us is right?" Mindful of procedure, she told him, "I'd have to clear it with my supervisor, but I don't see why she would say no."

"She might not, but I will." Then, just in case the woman still had any doubt about what he was telling her, Colin said, "No."

"But, Officer…" Rebounding quickly, Miranda tried again. "…it's Christmas."

Colin's eyes narrowed. "It's November," he corrected.

"*Almost* Christmas," she amended.

The woman just wouldn't give up, he thought, his irritation growing to astounding levels.

"Look, why don't you get back into your car and drive off before I decide to change my mind about issuing you that ticket?" Colin suggested tersely. "You said something about a birthday party for a little girl named Lily," he reminded her.

"Oh my goodness! Lily!" Miranda cried, genuinely upset. She'd gotten so caught up with her idea about having the police officer visit the children in the oncology ward that she'd forgotten the mission she was on right now. "The poor thing's going to really be upset if I don't turn up on time."

Whirling around, Miranda hurried back to her car and got in. She was starting the vehicle before she even closed the door.

Raising his voice, Colin called after her, "Remember the speed limit!"

There was next to no traffic at the moment.

Reining herself in, knowing that the officer would be

watching her pull away from the curb, Miranda gripped the steering wheel and drove off at a respectable speed, all the while wishing herself already at her destination.

Despite her hurry to get to the women's shelter, she made a mental note to track down the officer and get his name and number from his precinct the first chance she got. This wasn't over yet, she promised herself.

Miranda managed to catch all the lights and breeze through them, arriving at the women's shelter fifteen minutes later.

Rather than wasting time driving around and looking for a parking spot near the gray, two-story building's front door, she pulled into the first space she came to.

Grabbing the cake, she hurried into the building— and nearly collided with the blonde little girl who was anxiously waiting for her at the door.

"You came!" Lily cried happily, her furrowed brow smoothing out the second she saw Miranda.

"Of course I came," she said, pausing to kiss the top of Lily's head as she balanced the large cake box in her arms. "I told you I would. It's your birthday and I wouldn't miss that for the world."

Lily was all but dancing on her toes, eagerly looking at the rectangular box in Miranda's arms. "Is that a cake?"

"Aw, you guessed," Miranda said, pretending to be disappointed that her secret had been uncovered. "What gave it away?"

"The box," Lily answered solemnly, as if she'd been asked a legitimate question. And then she giggled as she added, "And I can smell cake."

"Well, since you guessed what it is, I guess you get to keep it," Miranda told her.

Lily was all but bursting with excitement. "Can I carry it to the dining room?" she asked.

That wouldn't be a good idea, Miranda thought. The box was large and would prove to be rather unwieldy for a little girl to carry.

"Well, it's kind of heavy," she told her. "So why don't I carry it there for you and you can open the box once I put it on the table?"

"Okay," Lily responded, obviously ready to agree to anything her idol suggested.

The little girl literally skipped to the dining area at Miranda's side. And she never took her eyes off the box, as if afraid it would suddenly disappear if she did.

"What kind of cake is it?" she asked.

"A birthday cake," Miranda replied solemnly.

Lily giggled and waved her hand at her friend. "I know that, silly," she told her. "I mean what kind of birthday cake?"

"A good one," Miranda said, still pretending that she didn't understand what Lily was asking her.

"Besides that," Lily pressed, giggling again.

"It's a lemon cake with vanilla frosting," Miranda told the bubbly little girl beside her as they reached the dining area.

Lily's eyes grew huge with obvious delight. "Lemon cake's my very favorite in the whole world."

"Well, how about that." Miranda pretended to marvel. "I didn't know that."

"Yes, you did," Lily said, a surprisingly knowing look on her small, thin face.

And then Miranda smiled affectionately at the girl. "I guess I did at that. Guess what else I've got," she said.

"Candles?" Lily asked in a hopeful whisper.

Miranda nodded. "Eight big ones. And one extra one for luck."

Instead of saying anything in response to the information, Lily threaded her small arm through one of her friend's and hugged it hard, her excitement all but palpable.

Miranda could feel her heart practically squeezing within her chest. This moment she was sharing with Lily was both humbling and sad. Other children her age would have asked for toys or expensive video games, and not shown half the excitement when they received them that Lily displayed over the fact that she was getting a birthday cake—with candles.

Drawn by the sound of Lily's squeals, Amelia Sellers, the tall, angular-looking woman who ran the shelter, made her way over to them. Her smile was warm and genuine—and perhaps slightly relieved, as well.

Amelia'd probably thought she wasn't going to make it. Most likely because she had a habit of being early, not running late like this.

"Lily's been looking forward to this all day," Amelia told her the moment she reached them.

"So have I," Miranda assured both the director and the little girl, who was looking up at her with nothing short of adoration in her eyes.

"I put out the plates," Amelia announced, gesturing at one of the dining tables. "So let's get started."

Miranda smiled down at Lily, who was obviously waiting for her to make the first move. She had to be the most well-mannered eager little girl she'd ever met.

"Let's," Miranda agreed.

Carefully taking the half sheet cake out of the box, Miranda moved the rectangular container aside and out of the way. She then put the candles on the cake, making sure she spaced them close enough together that Lily would be able to blow them all out at once when she made her wish.

The moment the birthday cake was placed on the table, children began coming over, clustering around the table, all hoping to get a piece.

Taking out the book of matches she had picked up when she'd purchased the candles, Miranda struck one and then carefully lit the eight plus one wicks.

Blowing out the match, she looked at all the eager faces around the table. "All right," she told the small gathering. "Everybody sing!"

And she led the pint-size group, along with the smattering of adults also gathered around the table, in a loud, if slightly off-key chorus of "Happy Birthday." All the while she kept one eye on Lily, who looked positively radiant.

When the children stopped singing, Miranda told the little girl, "Okay, Lily, make a wish and blow out the candles."

Nodding, Lily pressed her lips together, clearly giving her wish a great deal of thought. Then she looked up at Miranda and smiled.

Taking in a deep breath, Lily leaned over the cake and blew as hard as she could. The candles flickered and went out.

"You got them all," Miranda declared, applauding the little girl's accomplishment.

The children and adults around the table joined in, some loudly cheering, as well.

Miranda felt someone tugging on the bottom of her tunic. Glancing down, she found herself looking into the upturned face of an animated little boy named Paul.

"Now can we have some cake?" he asked.

"Absolutely," she replied. "Right after Lily gets the first piece."

Removing all nine candles, she set them on a napkin. Miranda proceeded to cut a piece of cake for Lily, making sure it was an extra-large one.

Out of the corner of her eye she saw Lily folding the napkin over the candles she'd just removed. The little girl covertly slipped the napkin into the pocket of her jeans, a souvenir of her special day.

"There you go," Miranda told her, sliding the plate to her.

"Thank you," Lily said.

To Miranda's surprise, rather than devour the cake as she expected, the little girl ate the slice slowly, as if savoring every morsel.

"This is the best cake I ever had," Lily declared when she finally finished it.

The other children had made short work of the cake

that was left, but Miranda had anticipated that. "You can have another piece," she told Lily. Not waiting for a response, she pushed her own plate in front of the little girl.

Lily looked tempted, but left the slice untouched.

"What's wrong?" Miranda asked.

"I can't eat that. That's your piece," she protested.

Miranda smiled at the girl. *One in a million*, she thought.

Out loud she stated, "And I saved it for you. I wanted you to have an extra piece and knew that the rest of the cake would probably be gobbled up fast. So don't argue with me, young lady. Take this piece. It's yours," she coaxed.

Lily still looked uncertain. "Really?"

"Really," Miranda assured her. "I'm the grown-up here. You have to listen."

Lily's face was all smiles as she happily dug into the second piece.

When she finished, Miranda cleared away the plates, stacking them on the side.

"That was the best cake ever!" Lily told her with enthusiasm, and then hugged her again.

"Glad to hear that," Miranda said, when the little girl loosened her hold. "By the way, I have something for you."

"For me?" Lily cried, clearly amazed. It was obvious that she felt the cake was her big prize. Anything else was above and beyond all expectation. "What is it?"

Miranda reached into the oversize purse she'd left

on the floor and pulled out the gift she had wrapped for Lily early this morning, before she'd left for the hospital.

Handing it over, she said, "Why don't you open it and see?"

Lily held the gift as if she couldn't decide whether to unwrap it or just gaze at it adoringly for a while. Her curiosity finally won out and she started peeling away the wrapping paper.

The moment she'd done so, her mouth dropped open. "You got me a puppy!" she cried.

"Well," Miranda amended, "I can't get you a *real* puppy because the shelter won't allow it, so for now, I want you to have this stuffed one. But someday, when you're in a home again, I'll come and bring you a real one," she promised.

Heaven knew she had access to enough homeless dogs at the animal shelter to pick just the right one for the little girl.

Lily threw her arms around her a third time and hugged her as hard as she could. "I wish you were my mom," she said breathlessly.

Touched though she was, Miranda knew she couldn't have the girl feeling like that. "Don't say that, honey. Your real mom's out there and she's probably trying to get back here to you right now."

But Lily shook her head. "I still wish you were my mom," she insisted, burying her face against Miranda as she clutched the stuffed dog. "Thank you for my cake and my candles and my puppy. Thank you for everything," she cried.

Miranda hugged the little girl, moved almost to tears

and wishing there was something she could do for her beyond giving her a gift and a cake.

And then it came to her. She knew what she had to do.

She needed to track down the police officer on the motorcycle. Not to bring to the hospital with her—that would come later—but to help her find out what had happened to Lily's mother. The man had resources at his disposal that she certainly didn't have.

All she needed to do, once she located him, Miranda thought, was to appeal to his sense of justice or humanity, or whatever it took to get him to agree to look for Lily's mother.

Smiling, she hugged Lily a little harder.

Chapter Three

Because she didn't want to risk possibly getting the motorcycle officer in any sort of trouble by going to the precinct and asking about him, Miranda spent the rest of that evening and part of the night reviewing her viable options.

By the next morning, Miranda decided that her best course of action was to literally track down the officer. That meant driving by the overpass where he'd been yesterday. She could only hope that he'd be there, waiting to ticket someone going over the speed limit.

But when she swung by the area that afternoon, after her shift was over, the police officer wasn't there.

Disappointed, Miranda had to concede that not finding him there stood to reason. If an officer frequented the same spot day after day, word would quickly spread and drivers would either avoid the area altogether or at the very least be extra cautious about observing the speed limit.

Still, as she drove slowly by the overpass, Miranda wondered how far away the police officer could be. Unless he had been relocated, there must be a certain radius he had to adhere to, so as not to cross into another cop's territory, right?

Giving herself a fifteen-minute time limit to find him, Miranda drove up one street and down another. She knew she was attempting to second-guess a man she knew absolutely nothing about, but at the moment she couldn't think of an alternative.

Fifteen minutes later Miranda sighed. The time was up and she still hadn't found the officer. She didn't want to be too late getting to the women's shelter. She knew that Lily's mother still hadn't shown up—she'd called Amelia to check—and the little girl would be devastated if she didn't come to see her as she'd promised.

She had to go, Miranda thought. Maybe she'd come across the traffic cop tomorrow.

Slowing down, Miranda did a three-point turn in order to head toward the street that would ultimately take her to the shelter.

As she approached the red light at an intersection, a fleeting glint from the left caught her attention. The setting sun was reflecting off some sort of metal.

Miranda turned her head in that direction, and found the sun was hitting the handlebars of a motorcycle.

A police motorcycle.

His motorcycle.

Although the officer was wearing a helmet, and virtually *all* police motorcycles in Bedford looked alike, something told her that this particular officer was the one who had pulled her over yesterday. Pulled her over and didn't give her a ticket. Miranda could feel it in her gut.

When the light turned green, instead of driving straight ahead, she deliberately eased her car to the left, into the next lane. Far enough to allow her to make a left-hand turn.

As she did so, she rolled down her window and honked her horn twice. Getting the officer's attention, she waved her hand at the man, indicating that she wanted him to make a U-turn and follow her. She then mentally crossed her fingers that she hadn't accidentally made a mistake, and that this *was* the same officer she'd interacted with yesterday.

Always alert when he was on the job, Colin tensed when he heard the driver honking. Seeing an arm come out of the driver's window, waving to get his attention, he bit off a curse. Was the woman taunting him? Or did she actually *want* to get a ticket?

And then, as he looked closer, he realized that it was the same car he'd pulled over yesterday. The one driven by that petite blonde with the really deep blue eyes.

The one who had that birthday cake on the passenger seat.

What was she doing here? Was she deliberately trying to press her luck? Because if she was, she was in for a surprise.

Her luck had just run out, he thought.

Biting off a few choice words under his breath, Colin made a U-turn and took off after her.

Less than thirty seconds later, he realized that she wasn't going anywhere. The woman with the soulful doe eyes had pulled over to the curb.

Something was definitely off, Colin thought as he brought his motorcycle to a halt behind her vehicle.

Training from his days on the force in Los Angeles had Colin approaching the car with caution. Every police officer knew that the first thirty seconds after a vehicle was pulled over were the most dangerous ones. If something bad was going to happen, it usually took place within that space of time.

Ninety-nine times out of a hundred, the pulled-over driver was harmless. It was that one other time that turned out to be fatal.

Although he had volunteered for this detail, choosing to patrol the city streets on a motorcycle over riding around in a squad car with a partner, he was not unaware of the risk that came with the job. A risk that always had his adrenaline flowing and his breath backing up in his lungs for that short time that it took for him to dismount and approach the offending driver's vehicle.

If he had a partner, there would be someone close by who had his back. However, Owens, his last partner, had been killed on the job, and although Colin never said anything to anyone about it, that had weighed really heavily on him, and still did. After that tragic incident, he operated alone. Patrolling alone meant he had to watch out only for himself. He liked it that way.

The second he peered into the passenger window

and saw the driver, he knew that he was facing another kind of danger entirely.

No one was going to die today, but it was still a risk.

Miranda rolled down the passenger window and leaned toward him. "Hi. I wasn't speeding this time," she said, greeting him with a cheerful smile and a chipper demeanor he found almost annoyingly suspicious.

He scowled at her. "No, you were just executing a very strange turn."

"I had to," Miranda explained. "If I went straight and turned at the next light, by the time I came back, I was afraid that you'd be gone."

Only if I'd been lucky, Colin thought.

Just what was this woman's game? "And that would have been a problem because…?"

She never missed a beat. "Because I had to talk to you."

The idea of just turning away and getting back on his motorcycle was exceedingly tempting, but for some reason he couldn't quite put his finger on, Colin decided to hear this overly upbeat woman out.

"You are persistent, aren't you?" he retorted.

"You say that like it's a bad thing." Miranda did her best to try to get the officer to lighten up a little and smile.

His stoic expression never changed. "It is from where I'm standing." He'd glimpsed her driver's license yesterday and tried to recall the name he'd seen on it. Maybe if he made this personal, he'd succeed in scaring her off. "What do you want, Miriam?"

"Miranda," she corrected, still sounding annoyingly

cheerful. "That's okay, a lot of people get my name wrong at first. It takes getting used to."

"I have no intention of getting used to it," he informed her. *Or you.*

As far as he was concerned, the woman was really pushing her luck.

"Look, I let you off with a warning yesterday," he reminded her. "Would you like me to rescind that warning and give you a ticket?"

Colin was fairly confident that the threat of a ticket would be enough to make her back off.

"No. That was very nice of you yesterday. That's the reason I came looking for you today."

She wasn't making any sense. And then he remembered what she'd said yesterday about asking him to pay a visit to some ward at the hospital.

That's what this was about, he decided. Something about sick children. Well, he was not about to get roped into anything. Who knew what this woman's ultimate game really was?

"Look, I already told you," he retorted. "I'm not the type to come see kids in a hospital. I don't like hospitals."

Rather than look disappointed as he'd expected her to, the woman nodded. "A lot of people don't," she agreed.

Okay, she was obviously stalking him, and this was over. "Well then, have a nice day," Colin told her curtly, and then turned to walk back to his motorcycle.

"I'm not here about the hospital," Miranda called

after him. "Although I'd like to revisit that subject at a later time."

Colin stopped walking. The woman had to be one of the pushiest people he'd ever encountered, not to mention she had a hell of a lot of nerve.

Against his better judgment, he found himself turning around again to face her. "And just what are you 'here' about?" he asked.

There was absolutely nothing friendly in his voice that invited her to talk. But she did anyway.

"That little girl I told you about?" Miranda began, feeling as if she was picking her way through a minefield that could blow up on her at any moment. "The one with your aunt's name," she reminded him, hoping that would get the officer to listen, and buy her a little more time.

"Lily," he repeated, all but growling the name. "What about her?" he asked grudgingly.

He wasn't a curious man by any stretch of the imagination, but there was something about this overly eager woman that had him wondering just where she was taking this.

"Lily's mother is missing," she told him, never taking her eyes off his face.

Rather than show some sort of reaction to what she'd just said, his expression never changed. He looked, Miranda thought, as if she'd just given him a bland weather report.

She began to wonder what had damaged the man to this extent.

"So go to the precinct and report it," Colin told her. "That's the standard procedure."

"The director at the shelter already did that," Miranda answered.

"All right, then it's taken care of." What more did she expect him to do? Colin wondered irritably as he began to walk away again.

"No, it isn't," Miranda insisted, stepping out of her car and moving quickly between him and his motorcycle. "The officer who took down the information said that maybe Lily's mother took off. He said a lot of women in her situation feel overwhelmed and just leave. He said that maybe she'd come to her senses in a few days and return for her daughter."

"Okay, you have your answer," Colin said, moving around this human roadblock.

Again Miranda shifted quickly so he couldn't get to his motorcycle. She ignored the dark look he gave her. She wasn't about to give up. This was important. Lily was depending on her to do everything she could to find her mother.

"But what if she doesn't?" Miranda asked. "What if she didn't take off? What if something's happened to Lily's mother and that's why she never came back to the shelter?"

He felt as if this doe-eyed blonde was boxing him in. "That's life," he said, exasperated.

"There's a little eight-year-old girl at the shelter waiting for her mommy to come back," Miranda told him with feeling. "I can't just tell her 'that's life.'"

Taking hold of Miranda's shoulders, he moved her

firmly out of his way and finally reached his motorcy-cle. "Tell her whatever you like."

Miranda raised her voice so that he could hear her above the sound of the cars going by. "I'd like to tell her that this nice police officer is trying to find her mommy."

Colin turned sharply on his heel and glared at this woman who refused to take a hint. "Look, lady—"

"Miranda," she prompted.

"Miranda," Colin echoed between gritted teeth. "You are a royal pain, you know that?"

Miranda had always tried to glean something posi-tive out of every situation, no matter how bleak it might appear. "Does that mean you'll look for her?" she asked hopefully.

Colin blew out an angry breath. "That means you're a royal pain," he repeated.

With nothing to lose, Miranda climbed out on a limb. "Please? I can give you a description of Lily's mother." And then she thought of something even better. "And if you come with me, I can get you a picture of her that'll be useful."

He had a feeling that this woman wasn't going to give up unless he agreed to help her. Although it irri-tated him beyond description, there was a very small part of him that had to admit he admired her tenacity.

Still, he gave getting her to back off one more try. "What will be useful is if you get out of my way and let me do my job."

Miranda didn't budge. "Isn't part of your job find-ing people who have gone missing?"

"She's not missing if she left of her own accord and just decided to keep on going," he told the blonde, enunciating every word.

"But we don't know that she decided to keep on going. She did leave the shelter to go look for work," Miranda told him.

"That's what the woman said," Colin countered impatiently.

"No, that's what she *did*," Miranda stressed. "Gina Hayden has an eight-year-old daughter. She wouldn't just leave her like that."

"How do you *know* that?" Colin challenged. The woman lived in a cotton candy world. Didn't she realize that the real world wasn't like that? "Lots of people say one thing and do another. And lots of people with families just walk out on them and never come back."

Miranda watched him for a long moment. So long that he thought she'd finally given up trying to wear him down. And then she spoke and blew that theory to pieces.

"Who left you?" she asked quietly.

"You, I hope," he snapped, turning back to face his motorcycle.

He sighed as she sashayed in front of him yet again. This was beginning to feel like some never-ending dance.

"No, you're not talking about me," Miranda told him. "You're talking about someone else. I can see it in your eyes. Someone walked out on you, probably when you were a kid. So you know what that feels like," she stressed.

He needed this like he needed a hole in the head. "Look, lady—"

"Miranda," she corrected again.

He ignored that. "You can take your amateur psychobabble, get back in your car and drive away before I haul you in for harassing a police officer."

Was that what he thought this was?

She had to get through to him. Something in her heart told her that he'd find Gina, She just needed him to take this seriously.

"I'm not harassing you—"

He almost laughed out loud. "You want to bet?"

Miranda pushed on. "I'm just asking you to go out of your way a little and maybe make a little girl very happy. If her mother doesn't turn up, Lily's going to be sent to social services and placed in a foster home. The only reason she hasn't been taken there already is that the director of the shelter agreed with me about waiting for her mom to come back. The director bought us a little time." And that time was running out, Miranda added silently.

"The kid can still be taken away," Colin pointed out. "Her mother abandoned her."

Why couldn't she get through to this officer? "Not if something happened to her and she's unable to get back."

Colin sighed. He knew he should just get on his motorcycle and ride away from this woman. For the life of him, he didn't know why he was allowing himself to get involved in this.

"Did you call all the hospitals?"

She nodded. "All of them. There's no record of anyone fitting Gina's description coming in on her own or being brought in."

So what more did this woman want him to do? "Well then—"

"But there could be other reasons she hasn't come back," she insisted. "Gina could have been abducted, or worse." Miranda looked at him with eyes that were pleading with him to do something.

Colin shook his head. "I should have given you that ticket yesterday," he told her gruffly.

He was weakening; she could just feel it. "But you didn't because you're a good man."

"No, because I should have had my head examined," he grumbled. "All right," he relented, taking out his ticket book and flipping to an empty page.

Miranda's eyes widened. "You're writing me a ticket?" she asked.

"No, I'm taking down this woman's description. You said you'd give it to me. Now, what is it?" Colin demanded.

"What did you say your name was?" she asked.

"I didn't." He could feel her looking at him. Swallowing a couple choice words, he said, "Officer Colin Kirby."

"Thank you, Officer Colin Kirby."

Maybe he was losing his mind, but he could swear he could *feel* her smile.

"The description?" he demanded.

Miranda lost no time in giving it to him.

Chapter Four

"Okay," Colin said, closing his ticket book and putting it away. "I'll check with the other officer your director talked to. What's his name or badge number?" he asked.

Miranda shook her head. She hadn't thought to ask for that information when the director had given her an update. "I'm afraid Amelia didn't mention either one."

Colin looked at her. The name meant nothing to him. "Amelia?"

"Amelia Sellers," Miranda specified. "That's the shelter's director. She didn't give me the officer's name, but seemed pretty upset that he wasn't taking the situation seriously."

Colin read between the lines. He assumed that the officer the shelter director had talked to hadn't told her that he would get back to her. Not that he blamed the man.

"I take it this Amelia isn't as pushy as you," he commented.

Miranda wasn't exactly happy with his description, but the situation was far too important for her to get sidelined by something so petty.

"Actually, she can be very forceful. But the officer taking down the information really didn't seem to think that Gina was missing," Miranda said.

She was looking at him with the kind of hopeful eyes that made men seriously consider leaping tall buildings in a single bound and bending steel with their bare hands in an attempt to impress her.

If he was going to interact with this woman for any length of time, he was going to have to remember to avoid looking into her eyes, Colin told himself. They were far too distracting.

"I bet you were prom queen, weren't you?" he asked.

The question came out of the blue and caught her completely off guard. It took Miranda a moment to collect herself and answer, "Actually, I didn't go to the prom."

"No one asked you?" He found that rather hard to believe. She struck him as the epitome of a cheerleader. Was she pulling his leg?

Miranda didn't answer his question directly. She actually had been asked, just hadn't said yes.

"I had a scheduling problem," she said vaguely. "The prom interfered with my volunteer work."

"In high school?" Colin asked incredulously.

"You look surprised," she noted, then told him, "People in high school volunteer for things." At least, the people she'd kept company with had.

Shrugging, he said, "If you say so." He'd never concerned himself with social activities, even back then, nor did he involve himself with any kind of volunteer work. Most of his life he'd been a loner.

Securing the ticket book in his back pocket, he told her, "I'll see what I can find out."

"Don't you want the phone number at the shelter?"

He caught himself thinking fleetingly that he'd rather have her number. The next second he deliberately pushed the thought away. If he had her number, that might very well lead to complications, which was the very *last* thing he wanted. He supposed that obtaining the shelter's number was innocuous enough. Most likely if he used it he'd wind up speaking to the director.

"Right," Colin answered, doing his best to exercise patience. "So what is it?"

Miranda gave him the number to the shelter's landline, then waited for him to take out the ticket book again so he could jot it down.

Sensing what she wanted, he did just that. As he put the book away a second time he heard her asking, "Aren't you going to follow me to the shelter?"

It just didn't end with her, did it? he thought, exasperated. "Why would I want to do that?"

"To see Gina's picture," she reminded him. "I told you that there's one at the shelter. Lily has it."

He looked at her blankly for a split second until the information clicked into place. "Lily. Right, the little girl."

For a moment, he thought about telling her—again—that this wasn't something he did. His main sphere of expertise was keeping the flow of traffic going at a reasonable rate.

There were patrol officers who took this kind of information down, as well as detectives back at the precinct who specialized in missing persons. But he had no desire to get into all that with her. It would just lead to another prolonged debate.

Besides, it wasn't as if leaving the area was tantamount to abandoning a hub of vehicular infractions and crimes. And how long would following her to the shelter and getting that photograph of the runaway mother take, anyway?

Making no effort to suppress the sigh that escaped his lips, he said, "Okay, lead the way."

The officer's answer surprised her. She'd expected more resistance from him. Finally!

Her mouth curved. "So then, you are going to follow me?"

The woman had a magnetic, not to mention hypnotic, smile. He forced himself to look away.

"That's what 'lead the way' usually means," he answered shortly.

"I know that," she acknowledged. "It's just that I realize I'm asking you to go above and beyond the call of duty."

And yet here you are, asking me, he thought, irritated. Colin was beginning to think that the woman could just go on talking indefinitely. He, on the other hand, wanted to get this over with as soon as possible.

"Just get in your car and drive, Miranda," he instructed gruffly.

Her mouth quirked in another smile that made him think of the first ray of sunshine coming out after a storm. "You remembered."

"Yeah," Colin said shortly. He wasn't about to tell her that, like it or not—and he didn't—this fleeting contact with her had already left a definite imprint on his brain. "Well?" he prodded, when she continued standing there. "I don't have all day."

"Right."

The next moment she was hurrying back to her vehicle. Getting in, she started up the engine mindful of the fact that she had to be careful to observe *all* the rules. She had no doubt that if she exceeded the speed limit—and there seemed to be a different one posted on each long block—the officer behind her wouldn't hesitate to give her a ticket this time.

He'd probably see it as a reward for humoring her, Miranda thought.

But it didn't matter. She'd gotten him to agree, however grudgingly, to try to find Lily's mother, and that was all that *did* matter.

The shelter wasn't far away. Parking near the entrance, she got out of her car and stood beside it, waiting for the officer to pull into the parking lot.

When he did, he found a spot several rows away from her.

She watched him stride toward her. The dark-haired officer was at least six-one, maybe a little taller, and moved like one of those strong, silent heroes straight out of the Old West. She sincerely hoped that he would turn out to be Lily's hero.

"You've got ten minutes," Colin told her the moment he reached her.

He expected her to protest being issued a time limit. But she surprised him by saying, "Then I'd better make the most of it. Lily will probably be in the common area," she added. "That's where she watches for me to arrive."

"You come every day?" he questioned. Didn't this woman have a social life? He would have expected someone who looked the way she did to have a very busy one.

"I come here four, sometimes five days a week," she told him matter-of-factly. "Other days I work at the animal shelter, exercising the dogs."

Nobody did that much volunteering, he thought, opening the door and holding it for her. She had to be putting him on.

"What do you do when you're not earning your merit badges?" he asked sarcastically.

"Sleep," she answered, without missing a beat.

She sounded serious, but he still wasn't sure if he was buying this saint act. He was about to ask the woman if her halo was on too tight, cutting off the circulation to her brain, but he never got the chance. She'd turned away from him, her attention shifting to the little blonde girl who was charging toward her.

"There she is," Miranda declared, opening her arms just in time.

The next second she was closing them around the

pint-size dynamo, who appeared to be hugging her for all she was worth.

"Did you find her?" the little girl cried eagerly, her high-pitched voice partially muffled against Miranda's hip. "Did you find my mommy?"

"Not yet, darling," Miranda answered.

Slowly, she moved the little girl back just far enough to be able to see the man she'd brought with her. "But this nice officer—" she nodded toward Colin "—is going to help us find her."

Colin noted that the firebrand who had dragged him here hadn't used the word *try*. She'd gone straight to the word *help*, making it sound as if it would be just a matter of time before he located this missing mother who might or might not have taken off for parts unknown of her own free will.

He didn't like being tied to promises he had absolutely no control over, nor did he like deceiving people into thinking he could deliver on goods that he had no way of knowing he could even locate.

But when he began to say as much to the little girl, he found himself looking down into incredible blue eyes that were brimming with more hope than he recalled seeing in a long, long time.

How could this kid exist in a place like this and still have hope? he wondered.

"Are you going to find her?" Lily asked, all four feet of her practically vibrating with excitement and anticipation. "Are you going to find my mommy?"

"I'm—" He started to tell her that he would do what he could, because he wasn't in the habit of lying, not to anyone. Not even to children, who usually fell beneath his radar.

"Officer Kirby is going to need to see that picture you have of you and your mommy," Miranda said, cutting into what she was afraid the man was about to tell the little girl. "Can you go get it for me, Lily?"

The little girl bobbed her head up and down enthusiastically. "I'll be right back," she stated, and took off.

"I can't promise her I'll find her mother," Colin said in a no-nonsense voice.

"Maybe you could try," Miranda suggested. When she saw his expression darken, she tried to make him see it from Lily's side. "Everyone needs something to hang on to," she pointed out.

Colin looked totally unconvinced. "Hanging on to a lie doesn't help," he told her.

"It won't be a lie—if you find Gina," Miranda countered.

He couldn't believe she'd just said that. The woman obviously had her head in the clouds. "Does your plane ever land?" he asked.

"Occasionally," she allowed, and then, smiling, she added, "To refuel."

Colin was about to say something about the danger of crashing and burning if she wasn't careful, but just then Lily returned, burrowing in between them. The little girl was clutching a five-by-seven, cheaply framed photograph against her small chest.

Planting herself squarely in front of the police officer, she held out the picture for him to see. It was recent, by the looks of it, he judged. The little girl appeared the same in it and she was wearing the dress she had on now.

He caught himself wondering if it was her only dress, which surprised him. Thoughts like that didn't usually occur to him.

"That's us. Me and my mommy," Lily told him proudly. She held the framed photograph up higher so he could see it better. "Miranda says she's pretty," the little girl added. And then her smile faded as she asked, "You're not going to lose the picture, are you? It's the only one I've got."

Colin paused, looking at the small, worried face. "Tell you what," he said, pulling his cell phone out of his breast pocket. "Why don't I take a picture of your photo with my phone?" he suggested. "That way I'll have a copy to show around so I can find your mother, and you get to keep that picture for yourself."

He was rewarded with a huge smile that took up Lily's entire face. "That's a good idea," she told him. Her eyes were sparkling as she added, "You're really smart."

He was about to dismiss that assessment, flattering though it was, when he heard Miranda tell the little girl, "He's a police officer," as if the one automatically implied the other.

"Just seemed like a simple solution," Colin told the little girl evasively. "Now hold up the picture," he said to her, wanting to move on to another topic.

Lily did as he asked, holding the framed photograph as high as she could so that he had an unobstructed view. The moment he snapped the picture with the camera app on his phone and, after looking at the screen, pronounced it "Good," he suddenly felt small arms encircling his waist just below his belt and holstered weapon.

"Thank you!" Lily cried. "And thank you for looking for my mommy."

He was about to say that "looking" didn't necessarily mean finding, but before he did, something made him glance in Miranda's direction.

She was moving her head slowly from side to side, silently indicating that she knew exactly what he was about to say to the little girl, and imploring him not to do so.

Colin blew out his breath impatiently, then compromised and told the little girl, who still had her arms around him, "I'll do my best, Lily."

"You'll find her," she declared. "I know you will." Lily said it with the kind of unshakable belief that only the very young were blessed with.

"Lily, honey," Miranda prompted, "you need to let go of Officer Kirby so he can get started looking for your mommy."

"Oh."

He was surprised and maybe just a bit charmed, he discovered, to hear the little girl giggle.

"I'm sorry," she said, releasing him. "I just wanted to say thank you."

Again he wanted to tell her that just because he'd promised to *look* for her mother didn't mean that he was going to be able to *find* her.

Maybe it was because Miranda was standing so close

to him, or maybe it was all that hope he saw shining in the little girl's blue eyes, but the words he was about to say froze on his tongue, unable to exit. He couldn't bring himself to be the one to force Lily to face up to reality and all the ugliness that came with it.

So all he did was mumble, "Yeah," and then turn on his heel and begin striding toward the shelter's exit— and freedom.

It wasn't until he was way past the front door and standing outside, dragging in air to clear his head, that he realized the woman who had roped him into this was right behind him.

Now what?

Was she going to try to get him to pinkie-swear that he was going to come through on that half promise he'd been forced to make?

"Look, I'll do what I can," he said, before she could open her mouth to say a word.

To his surprise, the woman who was quickly becoming his main source of irritation nodded as she smiled at him. "I know. That's all anyone can ask."

No, Colin thought, as he mounted his motorcycle. The exasperating blonde was asking him for a hell of a lot more than that.

The thing that he *really* couldn't understand, he realized as he rode away, was that for some reason Miranda Steele was making him want to deliver on that vague nonpromise he'd just made to that little girl.

Chapter Five

He absolutely hated asking anyone for anything, even if it involved something in the line of duty. If he didn't ask, Colin felt that there was no chance of his being turned down. There was also the fact that if he didn't ask someone to do something for him, then he wouldn't owe anyone a favor in return.

Again he found himself wishing he had never pulled Miranda over to give her a ticket in the first place. If he hadn't done that, then he wouldn't be faced with the dilemma he was now looking at.

It was the end of his shift and Colin was tempted to just clock out and go home. But despite his desire to divorce himself from the situation, his mind kept conjuring up images of that little girl's small, sad face looking up at him as if he was the answer to all her prayers.

No one had ever looked at him like that before.

It was all that woman's fault, Colin thought grudgingly.

Miranda.

Who named their kid Miranda these days, anyway? he wondered irritably.

It was late, Colin thought as he walked into the locker room. Too late to really start anything today. To assuage his conscience, he decided to come in earlier tomorrow and maybe nose around, see if anyone had any information pertaining to a woman who matched this Gina Hayden's description.

After opening his locker, Colin took out his civilian clothes and began changing into them. He was tired and he'd be able to think more clearly tomorrow morning when he—

"The poor woman was lying there, slumped over by the Dumpster and hardly breathing. I thought she was dead. Really not the kind of thing you'd expect to see around here."

Colin stopped tucking his shirt into his jeans. The conversation that was coming from the row of lockers directly behind his caught his attention. He listened more closely.

"Lucky thing you found her when you did, Moran," a second, deeper voice commented. "Why did you go in that alley, anyway?"

Colin heard a locker door being closed before "Moran" answered the other officer. "I saw two kids running out of there. They looked pretty spooked."

"You think they were the ones who assaulted her?" the other patrol officer asked.

A second locker was closed. The officers sounded as if they were about to leave.

"There was no blood on either one of them," Moran was saying, "and frankly, they looked too scared to have beaten her that way. To be on the safe side, I snapped a picture of them as they took off. They ran into a building across the way. Shouldn't be all that hard locating them if I need to."

Colin closed his locker. What were the odds? he wondered.

At the very least, he needed to check this out.

Making his way to the next set of lockers, he was just in time to catch the two officers before they left the locker room.

"What happened to the woman?" Colin asked.

Officer Bob Moran looked up at him, surprised by the question. They knew one another vaguely by sight, but that was where it ended. They'd certainly never talked shop before.

"I called a bus for her," Moran answered. "The paramedics took her to Mercy General."

"Did you go with her?" Colin inquired.

Moran looked slightly uncomfortable. "No. It was the end of my shift and she was unconscious. I figured she'd be more up to giving me a statement tomorrow morning."

"What happened to her?" Colin pressed.

The fact that he was asking questions seemed to surprise the other two officers. Moran exchanged glances with Pete Morales, the second policeman, before answering. "Looked to me like someone stole her purse. I couldn't find any ID on her—or a wallet."

Colin took out his cell phone and flipped to the picture he'd taken of the photograph Lily had held up for him.

He turned his cell toward Moran. "This her?"

Bushy eyebrows rose high enough to almost meet a receding hairline. Moran appeared stunned. "Yeah, that's her, minus the swollen lip and the bruises." And then he looked at Colin. "You know her?"

He put his phone away. "No."

When he didn't volunteer anything further, curiosity had Moran asking, "Then why do you have her picture?"

Colin scowled. Granted, this wasn't exactly personal, but he still didn't like being put in the position where he had to elaborate. He preferred keeping to himself in general and answering questions only when he had no other choice.

But he didn't see a way out without arousing even more questions. Pausing for a moment, he finally said, "The woman was reported missing from a homeless shelter."

"That her little girl with her?" Morales asked, his demeanor softening as he looked at the child holding up the framed photograph.

"Yeah," Colin answered shortly. "Thanks for the information." Without any further exchange, he began walking away.

"You going to see her?" Moran called after him.

Colin didn't stop to turn around when he replied, "That was the idea."

"I can go with you," Moran volunteered, raising his voice.

Colin almost asked why, but supposed the other man's conscience had gotten the better of him. Or maybe Moran just wanted the credit. In either case, Colin didn't care.

"You've done enough. I'll take it from here." He kept on going, then slowed down long enough to throw the word *thanks* over his shoulder before he left the locker area.

He heard a somewhat confused "Don't mention it" in response.

Colin just kept on walking.

The last person in the world Miranda expected to see walking into the women's shelter that evening was the motorcycle officer she'd managed to talk into looking for Lily's missing mother.

Ordinarily, Miranda would have left by now, but she'd stayed at the shelter today to try to bolster Lily's spirits. Despite her normally upbeat, cheerful nature, it was obvious that the little girl was sincerely worried about her mother. The fact that several of the other children there had told her that her mother had "run away" and abandoned her didn't help any. Lily refused to listen to them.

"My mommy wouldn't leave me!" she'd cried. "She loves me!" The little girl was convinced that something had to have happened to her mom, preventing her from returning.

Miranda had stayed at the shelter until she'd finally managed to calm Lily down and get her to fall asleep.

She was just leaving when she saw the officer coming in.

One look at Colin's grim face had her thinking the worst—and fervently hoping she was wrong.

It was obvious that he didn't see her when he walked in. Miranda cut across the common area like a shot, placing herself in his path.

Trying to brace herself for whatever he had to say, she didn't bother with any small talk or preliminary chitchat. "You found her," she said breathlessly, willing him to say something positive.

Colin hadn't been sure Miranda would still be here, but she managed to surprise him by materializing out of nowhere.

"Yeah, I found her."

Miranda immediately felt her heart shoot up into her throat, making it almost impossible for her to breathe.

How was she going to tell Lily that her mother was dead?

Her mind scrambled, searching for words, for solutions. Maybe she could take Lily in as a foster parent, or maybe—

The woman standing in front of him almost turned white. That was *not* the sort of reaction he was expecting from her.

She also wasn't saying anything, another surprise, he thought.

"Don't you want to know where she is?" he finally asked.

The startlingly blue eyes widened more than he thought was humanly possible. "You mean she's alive?" Miranda cried.

"Well, yeah," he answered, surprised she was asking that. "If she was dead, I would have led with that."

"Dead? Somebody's dead?" an adolescent boy standing within earshot asked, instantly alert.

"Every single nerve in my body, for openers, Edward." Miranda blew out a shaky breath. "That's what I get for jumping to conclusions." She turned toward the police officer, who had just become her hero. Suddenly, tears were filling her eyes, spilling out and rolling down her cheeks. "You really found her," she whispered, clearly choked up.

"We've established that," Colin retorted. And then he looked at her more closely and realized what was going on. "Hey, are you crying?" he demanded, stunned.

Miranda pressed her lips together as she nodded. "Miracles make me do that," she told him hoarsely.

He wasn't sure if the miracle she was referring to was that he had found Lily's mother, or that he had bothered to look in the first place. Either way, he knew he wasn't about to ask her to elaborate. He was determined to keep communication between them to an absolute minimum—or as close to that as possible.

Digging into his back pocket, he pulled out a handkerchief and pushed it into her hand. "You're getting messy," he muttered.

Taking the handkerchief, Miranda smiled at him.

I see through you, Officer Kirby. You're not the big, bad wolf you pretend to be. You're a kind man under all that bluster.

Wiping her eyes, she asked, "What happened to her?"

He'd gone to the hospital to get as much information as he could before coming to the shelter. He knew there would be questions and he wasn't about to turn up unprepared.

Drawing her toward an alcove, he told Miranda, "From the looks of it, someone tried to rob her. When she held on to her purse, the thug decided to teach her a lesson. Doctor said she was pretty badly beaten. She was unconscious when they first brought her in," he added.

"But she's conscious now." It was half a question, half an assumption.

The woman had been just coming around when he'd gone to see her. "Yeah."

"Which hospital is she in?" Miranda asked.

"The paramedics took her to the one closest to where they found her," he answered. "Mercy General."

Miranda nodded, absorbing the information. Lily. She had to tell Lily.

She started to head toward the back, where some of the beds were located, when she stopped suddenly and whirled back around to face Colin again. Hurrying over, she caught him completely by surprise by throwing her arms around him.

Startled, Colin's ingrained training immediately had him protecting himself and pushing the person in his space away. But that turned out to be harder than he'd anticipated. For a rather willowy, dainty-looking woman, Miranda had a grip worthy of a world-class wrestling champion.

The second she'd thrown her arms around him, she'd felt Colin stiffening. She was making him uncomfortable.

Loosening her hold, Miranda took a half step back. "Thank you," she said.

He'd never heard more emotion stuffed into two words in his life.

Colin deflected the tidal wave of feelings as best he could. "I'm a cop. That's just supposed to be part of my job."

The smile on her lips was a knowing one, as if she had his number—which was impossible, because they were practically strangers. Still, he couldn't shake the feeling that his protest was falling on deaf ears.

"The key words being 'supposed to,'" she told him. "I didn't think you were going to look for her," Miranda admitted.

That made no sense. "Then why did you ask me to?" he asked.

Her face seemed to light up as she answered, "A girl can always hope." And then she grabbed his hand and said, "Come with me."

But Colin remained rooted to the spot, an immovable object. "Come with you where?"

"To tell Lily that you found her mother," she answered, tugging on his hand again.

But Colin still wouldn't budge an inch. "You can tell her."

Miranda was nothing if not stubborn. He had done the work and he deserved to get the credit, which in this case involved Lily's gratitude. "You found her. Lily is going to want to hear it from you. And then after you tell her, you can take us to the hospital to see Gina."

She had this all mapped out, didn't she? He didn't like being told what to do. "You're assuming a hell of a lot, aren't you?"

Miranda gazed up at him with what had to be the most innocent look he had ever seen. "So far, I've been right, haven't I?"

"Well, guess what? Your lucky streak is over," he informed her.

But just as he was about to break free and walk away, Colin heard a high-pitched squeal coming from the far side of the room. Looking in that direction, he saw a small figure with a flurry of blond hair charging toward him.

Obviously, someone had woken the little girl and told her he was here. She must have put the rest together on her own.

"You did it!" Lily cried. The next moment, she had wrapped herself around him like a human bungee cord. "You found her! You found my mommy, didn't you?" Tilting back her head so that she could look up at him, Lily gushed, "Thank you, thank you, thank you!"

Utterly stunned, Colin looked at the woman standing behind Lily. "How—?"

"It's not just the walls that have ears here," she told

him, beaming just as hard as Lily. She nodded toward the cluster of children who had been steadily gathering around them as if that should answer his question.

"Can we go see her now?" Lily pleaded. She looked from her hero to Miranda and then back again. "Please, can we? *Can* we?" she asked, giving every indication that she intended to go on pleading until her request was granted.

Looking at the officer's expression, Miranda made a judgment call. The man looked far from eager to go with them and he had done enough.

"Officer Kirby has to go home now, Lily. But I'll take you," Miranda said, putting her hand on the little girl's shoulder.

"And I'll drive," Amelia told them, approaching from yet another side.

The director had been drawn by the sounds of the growing commotion and just possibly by her own pint-size informant. In any case, the woman appeared relieved and thrilled at the news.

"Officer Kirby found my mommy," Lily told the director excitedly.

"So I heard," Amelia replied. Nodding at Colin, she smiled her thanks. "All of us here at the shelter—especially Lily—really appreciate everything you've done, Officer Kirby," she told him.

Colin wanted to protest that he really hadn't done anything. He certainly hadn't gone out of his way to find Lily's mother. The information had literally fallen into his lap and all he had really done was follow up on it.

But something told him that the more he protested, the more gratitude he would wind up garnering. His protests would be interpreted as being modest rather than just the simple truth.

So he left it alone, saying nothing further on the subject.

Instead, he decided that going home could wait a while longer.

Turning toward the director, he addressed her and the little girl who was jumping up and down at his side. "I'll lead the way to the hospital, since I know what floor Lily's mother is on."

He deliberately avoided looking at Miranda, sensing that if he did glance her way, he'd somehow wind up being roped into something else, and his quota for good deeds was filled for the month.

Possibly the year.

Chapter Six

"Wait!"

The order came from the head nurse sitting at the second floor nurse's station.

When the three adults and child continued walking down the corridor, she hurried around her desk and into the hall to physically block their path.

Surprised, Miranda told the woman, "We're going to see Gina Hayden. We won't be long," she promised.

"Clearly," the nurse snapped, crossing her arms over her ample chest. "Visiting hours are done," she informed them in a voice that would have made a drill sergeant proud. "You can come back tomorrow."

Lily looked stricken. "But she's my mommy and we just found her," the little girl protested in distress.

"She'll still be here tomorrow," the woman told her,

sounding detached. It was obvious she wanted them off the floor and wasn't about to budge.

Lily's lower lip trembled. "But—"

"Rules are rules, little girl," the nurse maintained stiffly.

Colin felt Lily tugging on his sleeve, mutely appealing to him for help. He made the mistake of looking down into her worried face.

Swallowing an oath, he took out his badge and held it up in front of the nurse so she couldn't miss seeing it. "But they can be bent this one time, can't they?" It wasn't a question.

The head nurse looked no friendlier than she had a moment ago, but she inclined her head and backed off—temporarily.

"Ten minutes, no longer. Ten minutes or I'll call security," she warned.

"No need," Miranda promised the woman. A small victory was better than none. Taking Lily's hand, she urged the little girl, "Let's hurry."

"She's in room 221," Colin told them gruffly.

They moved quickly. He followed at his own pace.

There were four beds in the room, two on either side. Lily's head practically whirled around as she scanned the room looking for her mother. Seeing her lying in the bed next to the window, she sprinted over.

"Mommy!" she cried happily, and then skidded to a stop as she took a closer look at the woman in the hospital bed.

Her mouth dropped open in surprise. Her mother

was hooked up to two monitors as well as an IV. The monitors were making beeping noises.

The scene was clearly upsetting to the little girl, as were the bruises she saw along her mother's arms and face.

Inching closer, Lily asked in a hushed voice, "Did you fall down, Mommy?"

Gina turned her head and saw her daughter for the first time. Light came into the woman's eyes and she tried to open her arms so she could hug the little girl, but she was impeded by the various tubes attached to her.

"Oh, Lily-pad, I did. I tripped and fell down," Gina told her daughter.

Miranda squeezed the woman's hand lightly, letting Gina know that she understood she was lying for Lily's sake.

"We were all worried about you," she told her. "But Lily never gave up hope that we'd find you."

The expression on Gina's face reflected confusion and embarrassment. "I don't remember what happened," she admitted.

"That doesn't matter right now, darling," Amelia said in a soothing, comforting voice. "All that matters is that you're here and you're being taken care of."

"Officer Kirby found you for me," Lily told her mother excitedly. Taking Colin's hand, Lily pulled on it to bring him closer. "This is Officer Kirby, Mommy," she explained, showing off her brand-new champion to her mother.

Eyes that were the same shade of blue as Lily's

looked up at him. They glinted with sheer apprecia-
tion. "Thank you."

"No thanks needed," Colin told her, then explained,
"It's complicated."

Miranda suppressed a sigh. The man just couldn't
accept gratitude, she thought. She wanted to call him
out on it, but this definitely wasn't the moment for that.

"We're out of time," she told Lily, as well as Amelia
and Colin. And then she explained to Gina, "We promised the nurse on duty to only stay for ten minutes because it's after hours."

"We'll come back tomorrow, Mommy," Lily promised her solemnly.

Miranda bit her bottom lip. She wouldn't be able to
come by with Lily until after her shift at the hospital.
She looked at the director, a mute request in her eyes.

Picking up the silent message, Amelia nodded oblig-
ingly. "See you then," she told Gina, then patted the
young mother's hand. "Feel better, dear."

Colin waited for the three females to file out of the
room before he started to leave himself. He almost
didn't hear Gina say, "Thank you, Officer Kirby."

Again, he wanted to tell the woman that he hadn't
been the one who had located her. But that would take
time and the nurse at the station had given every indication that she would come swooping in the second
their ten minutes were up. He didn't trust himself not to
snap at the nurse, which would undoubtedly upset the
little girl, and in his estimation, she had been through
enough.

So he merely nodded in response to the woman's thanks and left the room.

"Mommy has to be more careful," Lily said authoritatively as she and the three adults with her headed toward the elevator.

Miranda looked at the little girl as they got on. It wasn't entirely clear to her if Lily actually believed what she was saying, or if she was saying it so as not to let the adults with her know that *she* knew something bad had happened to her mother.

In some ways, she felt that Lily was an innocent girl; in other ways, she seemed older than her years. Only children were often a mixture of both.

"That was a very nice thing you did," Miranda told Colin once they reached the ground floor and got off the elevator. When he stared at her blankly, she elaborated. "Getting the nurse to allow us to see Gina."

The officer said nothing. There was no indication that he had even heard her, except for his careless shrug.

The man was a very tough nut to crack. And she intended to crack him—but in a good way. Miranda smiled to herself. Whether Officer Kirby knew it or not, he had just become her next project.

They split up when they reached the hospital parking lot, with Miranda and Lily going back with Amelia, while Colin headed for his vehicle, a vintage two-door sport car that was a couple years older than he was.

"Goodbye, Officer Kirby!" Lily called after him. When he glanced over his shoulder in response to her parting words, Lily waved at him as hard as she could. It looked as if she was close to taking off the ground.

Colin nodded once, climbed into his car and drove off.

Lily insisted on standing there until she couldn't see him any longer.

"He's a hero," she told the two women when she finally turned around and got into the director's car.

"Yes, he is," Miranda agreed.

A very reluctant hero, she added silently.

"Hey, Kirby, there's someone here who's been waiting to see you for some time now," the desk sergeant told Colin when he came into the precinct and walked by the man's desk.

It was past the end of his shift and Colin was more than tired. It had been two days since he'd led that little safari of females into the hospital and he'd assumed— hoped, really—that Miranda was now a thing of the past.

But the moment the desk sergeant said there was someone waiting to see him, he knew in his gut that it had to be *her*. Granted, it could have easily been anyone else; Bedford wasn't exactly a minuscule city and it felt as if the population was growing every day. But somehow he just *knew* it had to be the woman he had made the fatal mistake of pulling over that day.

The annoyingly perky, pushy woman he just couldn't seem to get rid of. She was like a burr he couldn't shake loose.

"Where?" Colin growled.

"Need your eyes checked, Kirby?" the desk sergeant asked. "She's sitting right over there." He pointed to the bench situated against the wall fifteen feet away.

Reluctantly, Colin sighed and looked in the direction the desk sergeant was pointing.

Damn it, he thought.

It *was* her—and she was looking right at him. It was too late to make an escape.

He might as well find out what she wanted.

Striding over to the bench, he saw her rise to her feet. The woman appeared ready to pounce on him.

Now what?

Bracing himself for the worst, he skipped right over any kind of a formal greeting and asked, "Something else you want me to do?"

Just as sunny as ever, Miranda thought, more convinced than before that he needed her to turn him around. "No, actually, I brought something for you," she told him, hoping that would get rid of the scowl on his face.

It didn't.

He needed to stop her right there, Colin thought, instantly on guard. "I can't accept any gifts," he told her. "The department frowns on its officers taking any sort of gratuities in exchange for services rendered, either past, present or in the future."

He sounded so incredibly uptight, Miranda thought. They'd crossed paths not a moment too soon.

"This isn't a gratuity," she assured him, trying to put his fears to rest.

He wasn't about to stand here exchanging words with her. For one thing, she was far better equipped for a verbal battle than he was. For another, he didn't have time for this.

"Whatever you want to call it—gratuity, gift or bribe—I can't accept it." He concluded in a no-nonsense voice, thinking that would be the end of it.

He should have known better. The woman had shown him that, right or wrong, she wasn't one to back off.

And she was clearly not listening to him but was reaching into the large zippered bag she'd picked up from the bench. Extracting something from inside it, she held up what appeared to be an eleven-by-fourteen poster board for him to look at.

It was a drawing.

"Lily drew this just for you," Miranda told him. She pointed to the blue figure in the center of the page. It was twice as large as the four other figures present. "In case you don't recognize him, that's you."

And then she proceeded to point out the other people in the drawing. "That's Lily, her mother in the hospital bed, Amelia, and that's me." Miranda indicated the figure in the corner, who was almost offstage, appearing to look on.

Colin couldn't help staring at the central figure. "I'm a giant," he commented, surprised that the little girl would portray him that way.

As if reading his mind, Miranda explained, "That's how she sees you. You are a giant in her eyes. Heroes usually are," she added.

The term made him uncomfortable. "I'm not a hero," he retorted.

"I hate to break this to you, but you are to Lily," she told him.

Colin continued looking at the drawing, still not taking it from her. His attention was drawn to the stick figure the little girl had drawn of Miranda.

"You could stand to gain some weight," he observed, still not cracking a smile.

"That's good," she responded, as if they were having an actual serious conversation. "That means I get to indulge in my craving for mint chip ice cream."

He glanced at her rather than the drawing, his eyes slowly running over her, taking in every curve, every detail.

"You don't look as if you indulge in anything that's nonessential," he told her.

She laughed. It was a melodic sound he tried not to notice.

"You'd be surprised," she told him. When she saw him look at her quizzically—most likely because she *was* thin—Miranda explained, "I do a lot of running around—at the hospital, at the women's shelter and especially at the animal shelter." They had her exercising the dogs, which meant that *she* was exercising, as well.

"Don't you take any time off for yourself?" Colin asked, positive that she was putting him on.

Miranda smiled. The man just didn't get it, did he? "The women's shelter and animal shelter *are* my 'time off' for myself," she stressed. "I like feeling that I'm helping out and doing something productive. It makes me feel good about myself," she explained.

He still wasn't completely convinced. "Did you ever hear the saying 'Too good to be true'?"

She tried to suppress the grin that rose to her lips. "Are you saying that you think I'm good?"

"You're missing the point of the rest of the saying," he pointed out. Taking a breath, he decided that this meeting was over. "Anything else?" he asked her, impatience pulsing in his voice.

"Well, since you asked—have you thought any more about visiting my kids at the hospital?"

She called them 'her' kids, not just 'the' kids. Did she feel as if they were hers? he wondered incredulously.

He should never have asked if there was anything else. "No, I haven't," he answered, upbraiding himself.

Not about to be put off, Miranda asked, "Well, would you think about it? Please?" she added. "Christmas is getting closer."

Why should that make a difference? Christmas had ceased to have meaning for him when he'd lost his mother.

"Happens every year at this time," he answered.

Miranda gave it another try. "Well, like I told you, I think it would do them a lot of good. Their lives are really hard and they don't have all that much to look forward to."

"And my visiting would give them something to look forward to?" he asked sarcastically.

She never wavered. "Yes, it would."

The woman just wasn't going to give up. He didn't like being made to feel guilty.

"I'll think about it," he said, only because he felt it was the one way to get her to cease and desist. And then he looked at his watch. "Don't you have to be someplace, volunteering?"

"Actually, I do," she said, slipping the straps of her

bag over her shoulder. "I promised I'd come by the animal shelter. There's this German shepherd that needs a foster home until she can be placed."

The woman was a relentless do-gooder. "Right up your alley," he cracked.

Miranda smiled at him. He saw the corners of her eyes crinkling. "Actually, it is."

"Then you'd better get to it."

"I will. Oh, don't forget your picture," she prompted. Picking up the poster board drawing, she forced it into his hands.

"Right," he muttered, less than pleased.

He was still standing there, looking down at the drawing, as she hurried out the door.

Chapter Seven

Colin frowned. He needed to have his head examined. He obviously wasn't thinking clearly.

Or maybe at all.

Why else would he be out here, parked across the street from Bedford's no-kill animal shelter, waiting for that overachieving do-gooder to come out?

As far as he knew, he was free and clear, which meant that he could go on with his life without being subjected to any more taxing, annoying requests.

So why the hell was he here, *willingly* putting himself in that woman's path again? Why would he be setting himself up like this?

It wasn't as if he didn't know what Miranda was like. He'd learned that she was the kind of person who, if given an inch, wanted not just a mile but to turn it into an entire freeway.

Colin sighed. Knowing that, what was he doing out here?

Satisfying his own curiosity, he supposed.

A curiosity, he reminded himself, he hadn't even been aware of possessing a short while ago—not until life had thrown that woman into his path and she'd come charging at him like some kind of undersized, stampeding unicorn.

Damn it, go home, Kirby, he ordered himself, straightening up beside his vehicle. *Go home before anyone mistakes you for some kind of stalker and calls someone from the department on you.*

He'd talked himself out of being here and was just about to open his car door when he heard the sound of metal scraping on concrete across the street. A second later, he realized that the gates in front of the animal shelter were being opened.

Someone was coming out.

Colin's suspicions were confirmed a heartbeat later when he heard someone calling his name.

"Officer Kirby, is that you?"

He froze.

You should have been faster, he upbraided himself. Better yet, he shouldn't have been here to begin with.

Caught, he turned around, to see Miranda hurrying across the street toward him.

She wasn't alone.

She had a lumbering, overly excited German shepherd running with her. Miranda appeared to be hanging on to the leash for dear life. At first glance, it was difficult to say exactly who had who in tow.

Both woman and dog reached him before he had a chance to finish his thought.

Her four-footed companion suddenly reared up on its hind legs and came within an inch of planting a pair of powerful-looking front paws against his chest.

"You sure you can handle him?" Colin asked, far from pleased and moving back just in time to escape the encounter.

"Her," Miranda corrected, tugging harder on the leash. "It's a her."

That, in his opinion, was not the point. Whether the animal was too much for her was.

"Whatever." He never took his eyes off the dog. "You look like you've met your match," he told her as he took another step back.

"Down, Lola," Miranda ordered in an authoritative voice. The mountain of a dog immediately dropped to all four legs, resuming her initial position. "Good girl," Miranda praised, petting the German shepherd's head while continuing to maintain a firm hold on the leash with her other hand. Her attention shifted to Colin. "You're not afraid of a frisky puppy, are you, Officer?"

Colin continued eyeing the animal cautiously. "That all depends on whether or not that 'puppy' is bigger than I am."

"Don't let Lola scare you," Miranda told him. "She was just excited to see you." She petted the dog again. Lola seemed to curl into her hand. "I think she sees everyone as a potential master."

"Uh-huh." He wasn't all that sure he was buying this. Colin continued to regard the dog warily.

"Heel, Lola," she ordered, when the dog started to move in Colin's direction again. When Lola obeyed, Miranda looked at the police officer, wondering what he was doing here. This was not his usual patrolling area, and he was out of uniform. "Were you waiting for me, Officer Kirby?" she asked.

The expression on her face was nothing short of amused. A week ago, seeing an expression like that, seemingly at his expense, would have been enough for him to take offense, but for some reason now, he didn't.

Instead, he let it ride. Reaching into the back seat of his car, he took out the drawing she'd given him the other day at the precinct. "I came by to give you this."

Lola's ears perked up and the animal looked as if she was debating whether or not the drawing he was holding was something to eat.

Miranda pulled a little on the leash, drawing the dog back.

"That's not for you, Lola," she informed the eager German shepherd. Her eyes shifted back to the police officer. "Why are you giving it to me?" she asked. "Lily drew it for you. She wanted you to have it. It was her way of saying thank you."

Colin shrugged. "Yeah, well, I don't have anyplace to put it," he told her, still holding out the drawing.

He kept one eye on the German shepherd to make sure Lola didn't grab a chunk out of the poster board. He didn't want it, but there was no reason to let it be destroyed.

Holding the dog's leash tightly, Miranda made no effort to take the drawing from him. Instead, she looked at the tall, imposing police officer. The solemn expression in his eyes convinced her more than ever that the man needed fixing.

"You don't have any closets?"

"Of course I have closets," he retorted. What kind of question was that? Did she think he lived in a public park?

"Well, you could put the drawing in one of your closets," she suggested helpfully. "That is, if you don't want to hang it on your refrigerator."

Still not taking it from him, she glanced at the drawing. Thinking back, Miranda could remember producing something like that herself when she was younger than Lily. Hers had been of her parents and herself—and Daisy, her father's beloved Doberman. That had stayed on display on the fridge for almost a year.

"Most people put artwork like that on their refrigerator," she added, smiling encouragingly. This was all undoubtedly alien to him. "You must be new at this."

Colin furrowed his brow in concentration as he wondered what made this woman tick—and why she seemed to have singled him out like this. "I guess I'm new at a lot of things," he observed.

Her smile turned almost dazzling. "Hey, even God had a first day."

He thought of the last few days since he'd run into this sorceress. She made him behave in a manner that was completely foreign to his normal mode of operation. Exactly what was this secret power she seemed to have that caused him to act so out of character?

"Not like this," he murmured under his breath.

He heard Miranda laugh in response. The sound was light, breezy, reminding him of the spring wind that was still three months away.

For some reason, an image of bluebells in his mother's garden flashed through his mind, catching him completely by surprise. He hadn't thought of his mom's garden for more than twenty-two years.

He shook his head, as if to free himself of the memory and the wave of emotion that came with it. Colin felt as if he was getting all turned around.

"Is something wrong, Officer?" Miranda asked, concerned.

"You mean other than the fact that I should be home nursing a beer, instead of standing out here trying to make you take back this drawing?" Colin asked, exasperated.

"It's not my drawing to take," Miranda reminded him. "Lily wanted you to have it." And then she abruptly switched subjects. "Seriously? A beer?" she asked. "What about dinner?"

Colin stared at her. "Is this mothering-smothering thing of yours just something that spills out without warning, or do you have to summon it?" he asked.

She ignored his question. Instead, she made a quick judgment call.

"Tell you what," she said. "I owe you a dinner. Why don't you come on over to my place and I'll make it?"

"What?" he cried, dumbfounded. There was no way he could have heard her correctly.

"I'd offer to come over to your place and make dinner there—you know, familiar surroundings and all that to keep you from getting skittish—but I've got a feeling the only things in your refrigerator, now that we've established the fact that you have one, are probably half-empty cartons of ten-day-old Chinese take-out. Maybe eleven days."

He continued to stare at her, as close to being overwhelmed as he had ever been.

When she finally stopped talking for a moment, he jumped in and took advantage of it. "You done yet?"

"That depends," she answered, lifting her chin as if getting ready for a fight. "Are you coming?"

"No," he said flatly.

"Then I'm not done." Glancing at the dog by her side, she added, "I have a very persuasive companion right here who could help me make my argument. All things considered, I'd suggest that you avoid her attempts to convince you to see things my way and just agree to come along to my place."

Damn it, this was insane. But he could actually feel himself weakening. He really *did* need to have his head examined.

Colin put on the most solemn expression he had at his disposal. "You know, there're laws against kidnapping police officers."

Rather than back away, Miranda leaned forward, her eyes sparkling with humor. "Not if, ultimately, that police officer decides to come along willingly."

Then, as if on cue, Colin's stomach began to rumble and growl. Audibly.

Miranda smiled broadly. "I think your stomach is siding with Lola and me," she told him.

Colin scowled in response. She continued to hold her ground. He had to be crazy, but he found himself actually admiring her tenacity. If he had an iota of sense, he'd jump in his car and get the hell out of here.

But he didn't.

"That dog couldn't care less one way or another," he told her, thinking that might blow apart her argument and finally get her to back off.

She studied him for a long moment. Lola tugged on her leash, leaning forward as far as she could, but Miranda continued regarding the man before her, and seemed practically oblivious to the German shepherd. She was mulling over his response.

"You never had a pet when you were growing up, did you?" she asked Colin.

"Why would you say that?"

Miranda smiled. She had her answer. He hadn't told her she was wrong—which told her she was right.

"Because of what you just said," she murmured. "If you'd ever had one, you'd know that pets, especially dogs, *do* care about their humans."

He had her there, he thought. "I'm not her human," Colin pointed out.

"No, but at least for now, I am, and I care about you," she told him. "Lola picked up on that."

That was all so wrong, he didn't even know where to start.

"First of all, you said you were probably going to take a German shepherd home to give him—*her*—" he corrected, "a foster home. That means you're taking this dog home for the first time. She doesn't know a thing about you and she's not really your dog yet," he stressed. "And second of all—or maybe this should be first—" he said pointedly, "why the hell should you care if I have anything in my house to eat or not?"

Miranda never blinked once during what he considered to be his well-constructed argument. Instead, she looked at him, totally unfazed, and when he was done she asked, "Why shouldn't I?"

"Because we're *strangers*, damn it," he muttered in exasperation. "You don't *know* me," he added for good measure. Why didn't this woman *get* that?

In a calm voice, she went on to quietly refute his argument.

"You pulled me over to give me a ticket, then didn't after I explained why I went over the speed limit and where I was going." She paused for a moment, then told him what she felt in her heart had been his crowning achievement. "And then when I told you that Lily's mother was missing, you found her."

He felt like he was hitting his head against a brick wall. No matter what he said, she kept turning it into something positive.

"That wasn't my doing," he told her, repeating what he'd said the other day. "That all happened by accident."

Despite the fact that he had raised his voice, the woman just didn't seem to hear his protest. Or if she did, she wasn't listening. Instead, she went on to make her point.

"You came to the shelter to tell Lily her mother was at the hospital—when you didn't have to—and then you went out of your way to go with us to the hospital—when you didn't have to."

"Damn it, you're twisting things," he shouted.

At the sound of his raised voice, Lola pulled forward, as if to protect her.

"Stay!" Miranda ordered, stilling the anxious dog. And then she looked at Colin. "Why are you so afraid of having people think of you as a good guy?"

"Because I'm *not*," he insisted.

She inclined her head. "I guess we'll just have to agree to disagree on that point," she told him philosophically.

"*We* don't have to do anything," he retorted impatiently.

She smiled at him knowingly. "I think that you might see things differently on a full stomach. Here's my address," she told him, pausing to take a card out of her shoulder bag and handing it to him. "You might find it easier to just follow me," she suggested.

"I might find it easier to just go home," he contradicted.

About to cross back to her vehicle, Miranda stopped and sent him a smile that seemed to corkscrew right through his gut.

"No, you won't." She said it with such certainty, she stunned him. And then his stomach rumbled again. "See?" she said. "Your stomach agrees with me. Just get in your car and follow me. And after dinner, you're free to go home. I promise."

Heaven help him, she made it sound appealing. And he *was* hungry. Involved in a car chase this afternoon, he'd wound up skipping lunch, and his stomach was protesting being ignored for so long.

He shifted gears, going on the attack. "You know, it's dangerous to hand out your address like that," he told her.

Miranda smiled again, running her hand over Lola's head and petting the dog. "I'm not worried," she answered. "I have protection."

Colin decided to keep his peace and made no comment in response. He'd already lost enough arguments today.

Besides, he *was* hungry.

Chapter Eight

Colin nearly turned his car around.

Twice.

However, each time, he wound up curbing his impulse and talking himself into continuing to follow Miranda. He knew that if he didn't show up at her place for that dinner she seemed so bent on making for him, she would show up at his precinct tomorrow just as sure as day followed night. Probably with some sort of picnic lunch or something like that.

That was the last thing he wanted or needed.

Colin muttered a few choice words under his breath and kept going.

He might as well get this over with, and then maybe the book would finally be closed: he had done a good deed in her eyes and she paid him back with a dinner she'd made for him—hopefully not poisoning him in the process.

Caught up in his thoughts, Colin missed the last right turn Miranda took.

Watching his rearview mirror, he backed his vehicle up slowly, then turned right. When he did, he saw that her car was halfway up the block in front of him. Idling.

Miranda was obviously waiting for him to catch up.

Once he came up behind her, she started driving again.

His gut told him that he'd been right. There was absolutely no way this woman would have allowed him to skip having this payback dinner with her.

Her house turned out to be two residential blocks farther on. It was a small, tidy-looking one-story structure that seemed to almost exude warmth.

He caught himself thinking that it suited her.

Miranda parked her vehicle in the driveway. He parked his at the curb. It allowed for a faster getaway if it wound up coming to that, he thought.

She got out of the car, then opened the passenger door for the dog she'd brought home. Lola jumped down onto the driveway and they both stood at the side of her vehicle, waiting for him to come up the front walk.

"Don't trust me?" Colin asked, just the slightest bit amused, when he reached her.

"We just wanted to welcome you, that's all," she told him, nodding toward the German shepherd, which had somehow become part of this impromptu dinner.

Leading the way, Miranda went up to her front door

and unlocked it, then walked inside, still holding on to Lola's leash.

She threw a switch that was right next to the door. Light flooded the living room.

"Welcome back to your home, Lola," she cheerfully told the dog. After bending to remove the leash, she dropped it on the small table that was just a few feet beyond the entrance.

"She's been here before?" Colin asked. From what she'd said earlier, he thought Miranda was bringing the dog home with her for the first time.

"A couple of times," Miranda answered. "It was kind of a dry run to see how she fared in my house."

"And how did she?" he asked, shrugging out of his jacket as he walked into the house.

Miranda smiled. "Well. She fared well."

Colin was about to make a flippant comment in response, but he'd just glanced around and his attention had been completely absorbed by what he saw.

There was a Christmas tree in the center of the room. Not just a run-of-the-mill Christmas tree but one that looked to be at least ten feet tall. Overwhelming, the tree appeared to only be half-decorated.

The rest of the Christmas ornaments were scattered all over the room—in and out of their respective boxes—waiting to be hung up.

"It looks like a Christmas store exploded in here," he commented, scanning the room in total disbelief.

"I haven't had a chance to finish," Miranda explained. "I don't have much time left over every night to hang up decorations," she tossed over her shoulder as she made her way to the kitchen. "I'm usually pretty beat by that time."

Miranda was back in less than a minute with a dog bowl filled with fresh water and set it down in a corner by the coffee table.

"There you go, Lola, drink up," she told the animal. "Dinner will be coming soon."

Despite himself, Colin was surprised. "You've got a dog dish."

She paused for a moment to pet the dog's head. She viewed it as positive reinforcement. "Like I said, this isn't her first time here. And I believe in being prepared."

Obviously, he thought. Colin looked back down at the decorations that covered three-quarters of the living room floor space.

"Are these all your decorations?" he questioned incredulously. He'd seen Christmas trees in shopping centers with less ornaments on them than were scattered here.

"Well, if I'd stolen the decorations, it'd be pretty stupid of me to bring a police officer into my house to see them, wouldn't it?" she asked. Not waiting for a response, she told him, "Half these ornaments belonged to my parents. I've just been adding to the collection over the years."

"And the ten-foot tree?" Colin asked, nodding toward the towering tree. Most people opted for a smaller tree, if they had one at all. He couldn't remember the last time he'd put up a tree for the holidays.

"That was theirs, too. I inherited it. My mother decided that she needed to scale back and get a smaller tree. I couldn't see throwing away a perfectly good tree," she told him. Since he was asking about the tree, she said, "You can help me hang up a few of the ornaments after dinner if you like." Seeing the wary look on his face, she added, "But you don't have to."

The next moment, she turned back toward the kitchen.

"If I'm going to make that dinner I promised you, I'd better get started," Miranda announced. And then she caught him off guard by asking, "Would you like to keep me company?"

Thinking that she might ask him again to hang up ornaments if he chose to remain in the living room, he said, "Yeah, sure, why not?"

Miranda grinned. "That's the spirit. How are you at chopping vegetables?" she asked, moving toward the refrigerator.

"Depends on how you want them chopped," he answered drolly.

"Into smaller vegetables," she answered, her eyes sparkling with amusement. "I just want to be able to cook them faster."

Placing a cutting board and large knife on the counter in front of the police officer, she took three kinds of vegetables out of the refrigerator and deposited those in a large bowl. She put the bowl next to the cutting board.

"Have at it," she told him.

Colin regarded the items on the counter. "You didn't mention that I'd have to make my own dinner," he said.

"Not entirely," Miranda corrected. "It's just a little

prep work," she explained. "I figured you'd want to join in."

Cooking was something he usually avoided. Takeout and microwaving things was more his style.

"And exactly what made you 'figure' that?" he asked.

"Easy," she answered. "You don't strike me as the kind of person who likes standing around, doing nothing while he's waiting."

"I wasn't planning on standing, I was planning on sitting," he told her.

"You'll be sitting soon enough," Miranda promised cheerfully—in his opinion, *nobody* was this damn cheerful. What was wrong with her?

Turning away from the counter, she opened the pantry on the side and took out a medium-sized can from the bottom shelf. He assumed that whatever was in the can was going to be part of dinner. He watched her placing the can under a mounted can opener. Once the can was opened, he was surprised to see her emptying the can's contents into a bowl that was beside Lola's water dish.

She was feeding the dog.

"I take it that wasn't part of our dinner," he quipped drily.

Picking up the large knife, he made short work of the carrots he found in the large bowl.

She grinned at him. He deliberately looked away. "Not unless you have an insatiable fondness for ground up turkey liver."

"I'll pass," he told her.

"Hopefully, Lola doesn't share your lack of enthusiasm," she said, glancing over her shoulder toward the dog. The dog was eating as if she hadn't been fed for days, a fact that Miranda knew wasn't the case. She smiled as she watched. "Looks like she doesn't."

Lola was making short work of the liver that had been deposited in her bowl. Within seconds, the liver was almost completely gone.

A moment later, licking her lips, Lola looked up at her. She made no noise, but it was obvious what the dog wanted.

"Sorry, that's it for now, Lola," Miranda told her, walking away. "Play your cards right and you might get something later after we have our own dinner."

"If I were you," Colin commented as he went on chopping vegetables, "I'd consider myself lucky if she didn't destroy half those ornaments you have strewn all over the floor."

Miranda looked unfazed. "Lola's a good dog. She doesn't destroy things. Her philosophy is live-and-let-live," she told the policeman, taking out a large package of boneless chicken breasts from the top shelf in the refrigerator.

"How do you know that?" he challenged.

"I can just tell," Miranda answered, sounding a great deal more confident than he would have been, Colin thought.

Opening the package, Miranda proceeded to cut each of the individual breasts into tiny pieces with the shears she'd taken out of the utensil drawer. The pieces fell into a big pot that she'd put on the larger of the two front burners.

Watching her, Colin came disturbingly close to cutting one of his fingers with the knife that he was wielding. Sustaining a nick, he pulled back his finger just in time and then, swallowing a curse, he asked, "What are you doing?"

"Getting dinner ready," she answered simply, turning up the burner beneath the pot. Turning, she saw the tiny drop of blood. She took a napkin and attempted to dab at it, but he was not about to cooperate. "Do you want a Band-Aid?"

"No. I'll live." Taking the napkin from her, he wrapped a small piece of it around his finger only to keep the blood from mingling with the vegetables. "What *is* dinner?" he asked.

"Stir-fry chicken and vegetables over rice—unless you'd rather have something else," she offered, dubiously watching his injured finger.

The chicken pieces were already beginning to sizzle in the pot. "Seems a little late for that now," he told her.

Undaunted, Miranda shook her head. "It's never too late."

Colin got the distinct impression that the woman actually believed that—and that she applied it to life.

"Stir-fry chicken is fine," he told her. He was not about to have her start something from scratch. Who knew how long *that* would take?

His response was rewarded with a smile that reminded him more and more of sunshine each time he saw it.

The fact that it did bothered him to no end because he wasn't used to having thoughts like that. His was a dark world and he had gotten accustomed to that. This new element that had been introduced into his world disturbed the general balance of things and he wasn't sure what he was going to do about it if it persisted.

"Good," Miranda responded, stirring the chicken so as to make sure that both sides were browned. "Because that means that we're more than halfway to getting dinner on the table."

There was that word again.

"We."

He wasn't in the habit of thinking of himself as part of a "we."

Granted that he was part of the police department, but he was a motorcycle cop, which meant by definition that he operated alone. He was a loner and didn't worry about having anyone's back. "We" brought a whole different set of ground rules with it and he wasn't comfortable with those rules.

Coming here had been a bad idea, Colin thought. And yet, he wasn't abruptly terminating his association with this living embodiment of Pollyanna, wasn't walking out of her kitchen and her house. He was still standing here, in that kitchen, chopping vegetables like some misguided cooking show contestant.

Something was definitely wrong with him, Colin thought, exasperated.

"Perfect!" Miranda declared.

Taking the large bowl filled with the vegetables he'd just chopped, she deposited the entire contents into the pot. She stirred everything together, then poured in a can of chicken broth, followed by several tablespoons of flour.

Stirring that together, Miranda proceeded to drizzle a large handful of shredded mozzarella cheese into the mixture and added a quarter cup of ground up Parmesan cheese.

Watching her, Colin frowned. "That isn't stir-fry chicken."

"That's *my* version of stir-fry chicken," she clarified and then told him, "Give it a try before you condemn it."

"I'm not condemning it," he retorted. "I'm just saying that it's…different."

"And that's what makes the world go around," she told him with a smile.

Stirring the pot's contents again, she lowered the heat under the pot and turned her attention to making the last additive: the rice.

Measuring out two cups of water and pouring them into a small pot, she told Colin, "I do have a can of beer in the refrigerator. You're welcome to it and you can retreat into the living room if you like."

He glanced toward the living room and saw the German shepherd she'd brought from the shelter. As if on cue, Lola raised her head. He felt as if the dog was eyeing him, waiting for him to step into the room.

To what end?

He wasn't afraid of the dog, but why borrow trouble?

The next moment his mind came to a skidding halt. *Why borrow trouble?* That was a phrase he remembered his aunt used to like to say. He felt something pricking his conscience. He hadn't been to see his aunt for several months. He supposed he should stop by and pay the woman a visit. After all, it was getting close to Christmas and Aunt Lily *was* the reason he'd moved back to this city in the first place.

His aunt would probably approve of all this, he realized.

She'd approve of the decorations lying all over the living room, of the animal shelter dog hovering over the empty dog dish—and most of all, she'd probably *really* approve of this do-gooder-on-steroids who was fluttering around the kitchen, preparing some strange concoction that very possibly might just wind up being his last meal.

"Colin?" Miranda asked when he made no response to her suggestion.

Aware that he had just drifted off, he blinked and focused his attention on Miranda. "What?"

"Would you like that beer?" she asked again, nodding toward the refrigerator.

He glanced over his shoulder toward the living room again. The German shepherd was still looking straight at him. Colin shrugged indifferently.

"No," he answered. "I can wait until dinner's ready."

"Well, guess what?" she said, looking very pleased. "Your wait is over. Dinner is ready and about to be served."

Good, he thought, blowing out a breath. The sooner it was served, the sooner he could leave.

Chapter Nine

Miranda waited for what she felt was a decent interval but the silence continued to stretch out as she and Colin sat opposite one another at the small dining room table.

It was giving every indication that it would go on indefinitely. Even Lola remained quiet, sitting under the table close to her feet.

Finally, feeling the need to initiate some sort of a conversation between them, Miranda looked at her incredibly quiet guest and said a single word.

"Well?"

Colin glanced up at her and then back down at the meal he was presently eating. He assumed she wanted him to make some sort of a comment about the dinner she had served.

"Not bad," he told her.

"Coming from you, that's heady praise," Miranda

commented, amused. "But I wasn't asking if you liked the dinner."

"Seemed like it," he answered. And then Colin put down his fork and gave her his full attention. For a supposedly easygoing woman, she certainly didn't make things easy, he thought. "Then what *were* you asking?"

"I wasn't asking about anything specially. I was just asking for *something*—anything you might want to talk about. You know, most people make conversation when they eat."

He had no interest in what "most" people did. "I usually eat alone," he told her.

"It shows," she answered.

Okay, this had gone far enough. He'd let her feel as if she'd paid him back for the debt she'd mistakenly thought she owed him. But now this was over. It was time for him to go.

Putting the napkin on the table, he began getting up to leave. "Look, I—"

Miranda cut into whatever he was about to say and gave in to her curiosity by asking him, "Why'd you become a police officer?"

The question came out of the blue and caught him off guard.

He stared at her for a long moment, trying to make heads or tails of what was happening here. Was she actually asking him that or was there some kind of other motivation at work here?

"Is this an interview?" he asked sarcastically.

"I'm just curious, that's all," Miranda answered. "Being a police officer is all about 'protecting and serving,'" she said, referring to the popular credo. "You don't look all that happy about protecting and you just don't seem like the type who wants to serve."

He would have said the same thing, but life had a strange way of taking twists and turns. "What I am is someone who doesn't want to be analyzed," he told her curtly.

"I'm sorry, I didn't mean to sound like I'm invading your space, I'm just trying to understand you."

Her answer made no sense to him. "Why?" he challenged suspiciously.

"Because I'd like to be friends and friends understand each other."

"Friends?" Colin echoed, stunned as he stared at her. "We're not friends."

"Not yet," Miranda pointed out in her easygoing manner.

"Not ever," Colin corrected sharply.

He was resisting. Well, she hadn't thought this was going to be easy. "Everyone needs a friend," she told him.

He didn't appreciate the fact that she thought she had his number. She didn't. And if she believed that she did, she was way out of her depth.

"I don't," he snapped. Storming to the front door, he yanked it open.

"Yes, you do," she persisted softly.

If he stayed here a second longer, he was going to wind up saying things that he'd regret saying once he calmed down.

So he bit off, "Thanks for dinner," and left, letting the door slam behind him in his wake.

Miranda stood there, looking at the door for a long, long moment.

Maybe she'd pushed too hard. He was a man who needed to be eased into new situations, into accepting that being alone wasn't the answer.

About to turn away from the door, it occurred to her that she hadn't heard the sound of a car starting up—or pulling away, for that matter.

Curious, she opened the door and found herself looking up into the face of a man who was struggling to come to terms with the fact that maybe he had allowed his temper to flare and then spin out of control much too quickly.

Frowning, Colin mumbled, "I forgot to finish my beer."

"I didn't clear the table," she told him, then asked, "Would you like to come back inside?"

He inclined his head and rather than say "yes" he just followed her back into the house.

Still not ready to apologize or say that he shouldn't have just stormed out the way he had, Colin just asked, "Anyone ever tell you you're too pushy?"

Miranda pretended to consider his question as she walked back into the dining room.

"No," she answered. "Not that I know of."

He snorted shortly. "Then you're either not listening, or you're dealing with people who don't want to hurt your feelings."

"But you don't have that problem," she guessed, a smile quirking her lips.

Colin scowled. "My only problem seems to be you."

"I'll work on that," Miranda promised. And then she nodded toward his empty dish. "Would you like some more?" she asked.

"No, just the beer," Colin responded, sitting down again.

But Miranda wasn't finished being his hostess. "I have some ice cream in the freezer if you'd like to have dessert," she offered.

"Just the beer," he repeated.

"Just the beer," Miranda echoed, backing off for the moment. She smiled at him as she sat down again opposite him.

Colin shook his head. He'd just yelled at the woman and she was smiling at him. He just didn't get it. Blowing out an annoyed breath, he sat back and regarded her in silence for a long moment.

Then, still frowning, Colin forced himself to apologize.

"I'm sorry I lost my temper and yelled at you." This was a first for him. He wasn't used to apologizing.

"It's in the past," Miranda told him cheerfully.

He stared at her, trying to make sense out of what she'd just said. "Yeah. Five minutes in the past." Which meant, as far as he was concerned, that it wasn't in the past at all.

But he realized that wasn't the way Miranda obviously looked at things because she said, "Still the past.

And I'm sorry if you felt that I was invading your space. That wasn't my intention."

"Right. I know. You want to be friends," Colin responded, unable to fully cover up the exasperated edge in his voice. It frustrated him that he couldn't figure her out, couldn't get a handle on the woman.

Who talked like that? Or thought like that? Just what was her angle? There was no way all of this was genuine.

"Would that be so bad?" she was asking him. "Being friends?"

He felt like he was trying to get a sticky substance off his hands—and failing miserably no matter how hard he tried.

He tried one more time to make her understand. "Look, lady, we don't have a thing in common," Colin pointed out. "Not a single thing. You seem to see the world as this wonderful, shining place and I see it the way it really is."

"And how's that?" she asked him, wanting to hear what his answer was.

He never hesitated. "A dark place where everyone's out for themselves."

"I'm not," she told him.

He frowned. He had a feeling that she would say that. "Well, maybe you're the exception."

She'd expected him to say that and she was ready with a response. "And maybe there are more exceptions."

"Pretty sure you're the only one."

"What about your Aunt Lily?" she asked Colin pointedly. "Wouldn't you say that she's one?"

He eyed her sharply. "How do you know what my aunt's like?"

"Easy," Miranda answered. "When you asked me why I was speeding and I told you about being late for Lily's birthday, you said that you had an aunt by that name. One look on your face immediately told me you cared a great deal about that aunt."

"So now you're into face reading," Colin said mockingly.

"Not exactly," she corrected him. "You might say that I'm more into reading people."

Colin drained the last of his beer from the can and set it down on the table. He knew if he lingered, he was going to regret it. The woman was getting to him—and nothing good could come of that.

"I've got to get going," he told her, standing up.

Miranda rose to her feet, as well. Following her lead, Lola came to attention.

"Sure I can't talk you into hanging up a few ornaments with me?" Miranda asked. She was fairly certain that she knew his answer, but she wanted to ask just the same.

"Sorry. I'm totally out of practice," he told her as he started walking out of the dining room for a second time that evening. "I'd probably just wind up breaking them."

The way he said it had her drawing conclusions. "You don't have a Christmas tree?" Miranda asked.

"Not for a long, long time," he answered. "Thanks for dinner—and the beer."

She smiled as she walked him to the door. "My pleasure."

He shook his head. By all rights, she should be relieved he was leaving. He hadn't exactly been the kind of guest that a hostess kept asking to come back—and yet she was acting as if she'd enjoyed his company.

"You are incredible," he murmured.

Miranda's smile widened. "If I was incredible, I'd be able to talk you into coming to the hospital ward to visit my kids."

"You just don't give up, do you?" he asked in disbelief.

"What's the point of that?" she said. "If you give up, nothing happens. This way, there's always a chance that it might."

He made no comment on that. Instead, Colin merely shook his head. "There's such a thing as spreading yourself too thin, you know," he told her, trying to get her to be realistic.

There was that smile again, he noted. The one that told him she knew something that he didn't—and was pleased by it.

"Hasn't happened yet," she told him.

"Doesn't mean it's not going to." It was his parting shot.

He had every intention of going straight home. Heaven knew he'd earned it. Spending time with that chipper do-gooder had really tired him out. Hell, it had all but wiped him out, actually.

But it had also started him thinking. Not about Miranda and what was starting to sound like her endless tally of good deeds. What it had gotten him thinking about was the fact that he hadn't been to see his aunt since…well, he wasn't all that sure when the last time had been, exactly.

So rather than going home and having that beer that was waiting for him in his own refrigerator—a beer that would still be waiting when he finally did get home, he reminded himself—Colin rerouted his path and drove over to his aunt's house.

Of course, his aunt might be out, he told himself as he made his way there. But it was the middle of the week and Aunt Lily wasn't exactly the carousing type.

Colin pulled up in her driveway. If it turned out that she wasn't here, well, he'd tried, and according to that Pollyanna who had insisted on making him dinner tonight, trying was what counted.

After parking his car, he got out and walked up to the front door. It could use some paint. Maybe he'd come by and paint it for her over the holidays. He had a lot of time accrued because he usually didn't take any days off. There wasn't anyplace he wanted to go as far as vacations went, and staying home just meant he'd be alone with his thoughts, which was why he'd rather be working.

Colin rang the doorbell and waited.

He'd give it a total of ten minutes, and if Aunt Lily didn't come to the door by then, well, at least he'd—

"Colin?" The small, genteel woman standing in the doorway was looking at him in utter surprise. "Colin, is anything wrong?"

"No. Why would you think something was wrong?"

"Because it's Wednesday," she said. "I mean, because it's the middle of the week and you never come by in the middle of the week."

"Yeah, well, I don't really come by much at all," Colin admitted, feeling somewhat guilty about that. Especially since Aunt Lily never complained that she didn't see him.

"I know," she responded. Then, obviously realizing how that had to sound, she amended by saying, "I mean…" Reaching up, she touched his face lovingly. "You're sure nothing's wrong?"

"I'm sure." He laughed, shaking his head. "The only thing that's wrong is that I haven't been by much to see you."

"I understand, sweetheart. You've been busy," Lily told him. Wielding guilt had never been her way. Tucking her arm through his, she gave in to the sheer pleasure of seeing him. "Come in, come in. Have you eaten?" Not waiting for an answer, she offered, "Can I fix you something?"

"I already had dinner, Aunt Lily," he told her.

She closed the door behind him and then turned to look at her nephew.

"Today? You had something to eat today?" she questioned, then went on to say, "You look so thin."

"The department doesn't like to see fat motorcycle cops, Aunt Lily. It's hard on the bikes."

Lily shook her head. "It's a wonder they can see you at all. Are you *sure* I can't get you something to eat?"

In her own way, his aunt was as persistent as that

do-gooder was. "How about coffee?" he said. "I'll take some coffee."

"How about some banana cream pie?" Lily offered, preceding him to the kitchen. "You used to love banana cream pie when you were a little boy," she recalled.

He knew she wouldn't stop until he agreed to have something, and obviously coffee wasn't going to cut it. "Okay, I'll have a piece of pie. But I really just came by to see how you were."

Lily smiled. "I'm wonderful now that my favorite nephew's stopped by."

"I'm your only nephew, Aunt Lily," he reminded her, amused.

"That makes this that much more special.," She gave him one final penetrating look. "You're absolutely certain nothing's wrong?"

"Absolutely," he assured her.

"All right, then come to the kitchen and let's have some of that pie," she told him, hooking her arm through his again. Smiling up at his face, she said, "I've been dying for an excuse to have some—and this is certainly it."

"Glad to help," Colin told her.

Lily merely smiled.

Chapter Ten

Colin realized that he was more on edge and alert than usual. That was because he kept looking around for Miranda to pop up. He told himself that he *didn't* want to run into her. If he saw her coming, he could avoid her.

So he remained vigilant, expecting the woman to materialize somewhere along his usual route, the way she had the day she'd waylaid him about that little girl's missing mother.

He didn't drop his guard when he walked into the precinct, since she'd turned up there, as well.

But she didn't turn up there, nor did she track him down along his route. Not that day, nor the next day. Nor the day after that.

When the third day passed, he told himself he should feel relieved. That maybe "the curse" had been lifted.

But he didn't feel relieved. Instead, he had this uneasy, growing feeling of impending doom. He sensed that the second he let his guard down, Miranda would strike again.

The odd thing was that he felt edgier when she wasn't around than when she was and he was interacting with her.

So after the third Pollyanna-free day came and went, he began to think that something was wrong. Rather than leave well enough alone, he found himself needing answers in order to gain some sort of peace of mind—or a reasonable facsimile thereof.

Maybe she hadn't been around because Lily's mother had taken a turn for the worse. Or possibly that German shepherd Miranda had brought home with her—Lulu or Lola or something like that—had turned on her. It had been known to happen.

Not all German shepherds took after Rin Tin Tin, although Colin was still annoyed with himself for not just being grateful that she wasn't around, but actually seeking her out.

He refused to examine what he was doing, because if he had, he would have labeled himself as certifiably insane. What else would you call willingly leaping out of the frying pan into the fire?

As if in self-defense, he jabbed the doorbell before he could think better of it, get into his car and drive away as if the very devil was after him.

Run, you idiot! Get out of here before it's too late!

But he didn't.

He heard barking in the background the second he pressed the doorbell. Either that canine Miranda had brought home had turned into a guard dog, or she was trying to get his attention because something had happened to her mistress.

Damn it, what the hell was wrong with him? Colin wondered. He didn't *think* this way.

Calling himself a few choice names, he turned on his heel and began to walk away.

"Colin?"

Miranda had the same surprised note in her voice that he'd heard in his aunt Lily's when he'd showed up at her place.

Apparently nobody expected him just to drop in. So why was he doing it?

"Yeah." Colin answered almost grudgingly, half turning toward her. "I just wanted to make sure everything was all right—with Lily's mother," he added belatedly, not wanting Miranda to think that he was here checking up on her.

Knowing the perverse way the woman's mind worked, he'd never hear the end of it if she thought that.

Miranda's surprise gave way to a welcoming smile. "She's doing fine, thanks to you," she told him. She opened the door farther. "Why don't you come on in? Lola would love to see you," she added, glancing over her shoulder to the German shepherd, who was fairly leaping from paw to paw.

As if she knew that she had temporarily taken center stage, the dog barked at him.

Miranda laughed, then told her visitor, "And I've got some more beer in the refrigerator."

When he still made no move to come in, she took

hold of his arm and coaxingly pulled him across the threshold.

He should have made his getaway when he had a chance, Colin thought, allowing himself to be drawn in.

And then he thought of her offer. "Do you even drink beer?" he asked.

"No."

Okay, like everything else that had to do with her, that made no sense. "Then why do you have it in your refrigerator?"

That was easy to explain. She released him. "A few of the women I work with at the hospital and the animal shelter stop by on occasion. I keep the beer on hand for them."

Again Colin told himself he'd made a mistake in coming here. "I can't stay—" he began.

Miranda felt that maybe he needed to be coaxed a little more. "Well, you came all the way over here, so surely you can stay for one beer."

"It's not that far from your place to mine," he protested. His point was that he hadn't gone out of his way all that much—but he realized his mistake the moment the words were out of his mouth. He'd inadvertently given her too much information.

Her next words confirmed it.

"So you do live in Bedford." Not all members of the police department did. "What neighborhood?"

He was not about to compound his mistake. "There are stalking laws on the books, you know."

There was a knowing, amused smile on her lips.

"You're the one who showed up on my doorstep, and at the animal shelter before that," she pointed out.

He was immediately defensive. "Are you saying you think I'm the stalker?"

"I'm just saying it's only fair that I know where you live, since you know where I live." With a wink, she added, "Not everything has a hidden agenda. Sit," she told him. "I'll go get that beer."

When she walked back in, she saw that he was still on his feet and was looking at the Christmas tree.

"Haven't gotten very far decorating it, have you?" he commented.

Miranda handed him the cold can of beer. "Like I said, I only get to hang up a few ornaments every night. I can't seem to convince Lola to hang up any while I'm out." When his eyes narrowed and he looked at her, puzzled, she told him, "That's a joke."

"I never know with you," he admitted drolly.

She would have loved to just sit down beside him and talk, but she had a feeling he might think she was crowding him. It would seem more natural to him if she worked on the tree, so she asked, "Would you mind if I put up some decorations while you're here?"

Colin waved a careless hand. "Don't let me keep you." As Miranda got back to hanging up the ornaments, he took a long pull from the can. Lola had plopped herself next to his feet and looked up at him. The scene was far too domestic for him.

And yet...

"You decided to keep the dog?" he asked, assuming that was why the animal was still here.

"Well, at least until after Christmas," Miranda answered. Arming herself with several decorations, she moved around the tree, seeking out empty spaces. "Everyone who comes to the shelter at this time of year is looking for a cute little dog to give to their kids." She glanced over at the German shepherd and said fondly, "Lola's cute, but she definitely isn't little."

He laughed drily. "That's an understatement." He studied the animal. "She's got to be the biggest female German shepherd I've ever seen. I thought they were supposed to be a little smaller than this."

"Obviously Lola hasn't read the German shepherd handbook," Miranda quipped, stretching to hang up a long silver bell. "But what she lacks in daintiness she makes up for with friendliness. I've been working at the animal shelter for a couple of years now and she's got to be the most docile dog I've ever encountered." Picking up a few more ornaments, she searched for more empty spaces she could reach. "Most dogs freak out when they see a vacuum cleaner, much less when they hear one being operated. Lola, bless her, is completely indifferent to it. I could probably vacuum Lola and it wouldn't faze her in the slightest."

The dog wasn't all that easygoing, he thought. "I heard her barking when I rang the doorbell."

"That's because when she thinks someone is trying to come in, she instantly gets into her protective mode. She's being protective of me," Miranda explained, her voice coming from behind the tree. "Once she sees that I'm okay with you, she's fine."

Colin remained on the sofa, sipping his beer and absently petting the dog as he watched Miranda circling the Christmas tree, hanging up ornaments whenever she found a space.

"Damn," he heard her murmur under her breath. She'd worked her way back to the point where she'd started.

"What's the matter?"

She sighed. "I'm going to have to bring out a ladder from the garage to hang up any more of the ornaments tonight. The tree's beginning to look kind of bottom heavy and I can't reach the higher branches," she explained.

She was doing it again, he thought. Roping him into helping. If he had half a brain, he'd just ignore her.

Sighing, Colin stood up. Leaving his beer on the coffee table, he crossed to her. "Where do you want to hang that?" he asked, nodding at the decoration in her hand.

"Higher than I can reach," she answered.

Taking the decoration from her, he reached up to the branch that she'd obviously targeted and easily hung the ornament on it.

"That looks very nice," she told him, somewhat surprised that he had willingly volunteered to help.

"I wasn't exactly performing brain surgery."

"No," she agreed. "You were performing a service." And then she grinned as she held out another ornament. "You up for another one?"

"Yeah, sure. Why not," he said carelessly, taking the decoration from her and hanging it on the next branch over. Turning to face her, he saw the huge smile on

Miranda's face. "You're grinning like a little kid," he pointed out.

"Why shouldn't I?" she asked. "I've just witnessed a Christmas miracle."

Colin snorted. "Let's not get carried away here."

Her smile only grew; he didn't think that was possible, but it obviously was.

"Getting carried away is fun," she told him. "You should try it sometime."

The thought of doing just that—of getting carried away—popped into his head out of nowhere. It had nothing to do with hanging up decorations or anything even remotely along those lines. In his case getting carried away involved the sudden desire to find out what those smiling lips tasted like.

The thought zipped through his brain like a lightning bolt, daring him to follow through.

Okay, time to go, Colin thought sternly. He didn't know where that thought had come from, but he wasn't about to stick around and risk acting on it.

Turning his back on the tree and the miscellaneous ornaments that still needed to be hung up, he said, "Thanks for the beer—again."

Miranda looked at him in surprise. "You're leaving?"

"Yeah, I shouldn't have stayed this long," he told her. "I just wanted to find out how the kid's mother was doing."

They both knew that was just an excuse, but Miranda nodded as if she wholeheartedly believed what he was saying.

"Thanks for coming by," she said, walking alongside him to the door.

Colin stopped in his tracks. He didn't need an escort. Putting space between himself and the woman was the whole point of his leaving.

"I know my way out," he protested.

"I know that," Miranda answered.

Her tone of voice was friendly but firm, as if to let him know that she *wanted* to walk him to the door and wasn't about to be talked out of it.

As they approached the front door, Miranda began to broach another subject. "Since you're being in such a generous mood…"

Instantly on his guard, Colin looked at her warily. The woman seemed to know just how to get to him. He *knew* coming here had been a mistake on his part.

"Yeah?"

"The kids at the hospital would still love to see you," she told him.

"You just never give up, do you?"

Rather than be insulted or put off by his sharp tone and his question, she smiled as if she'd thought over what he'd asked. "What's the fun in that?"

He scowled. Maybe she thought of this as fun, but he certainly didn't.

He answered her seriously—and hopefully, once and for all. "I can't come to the hospital. We work the same hours."

"That's okay, I'll wait," she answered breezily. "Just tell me what time you can get there."

"Not until my shift is over," he snapped. "By then

you're on your way to one or the other of those two shelters where you volunteer." And that was that.

The next moment, he realized that he really should have known better.

"You know, the good thing about volunteering," Miranda told him cheerfully, "is that it's extremely flexible. There are no hard-and-fast hours for me to maintain."

Colin read between the lines. "I can't get out of this easily, can I?"

"You can." She certainly couldn't force him to come to the hospital. If nothing else, the man was a lot bigger than she was. "But between you and me, I don't think you really want to."

"So you've added mind reading to your list of talents, is that it?" he asked.

"No, no mind reading," she answered. "But as I said before, I can read people pretty well, and despite your bluster and your 'Big Bad Wolf' attitude, I think you're a good guy under all that."

Colin laughed wryly. "I guess it's a good thing you're not trying to earn your money as a mind reader. You'd wind up starving to death."

Her eyes met his—and then she gave him that soul-melting smile of hers. "So then it's a yes?" she asked innocently.

Every fiber of his being was geared up to shout "no" at her, that he wasn't about to be corralled or bullied into agreeing to turn up at a hospital ward like some sort of living, breathing show-and-tell object. He had absolutely nothing to say to one kid, much less an entire ward full of them.

But she was looking up at him with those eyes of hers, those eyes that despite all his attempts to shut them out seemed to get past all his safeguards and burrow right into him, giving him no peace.

"We'll see," he finally growled.

Miranda caught her lower lip between her teeth as if debating what to say next. "So that's a yes?" she asked again.

"No," Colin corrected, holding his ground. "That's a 'we'll see.'"

"Almost as good," she told him with more enthusiasm than he felt the phrase merited. The woman was incredible. She found optimism where absolutely none existed.

The next moment, she joyfully told him, "Thank you!"

With one hand on his arm to steady herself, Miranda rose up on her toes to kiss his cheek in gratitude.

That was the exact moment he turned his head to tell her that he hadn't done anything yet and most likely would not.

He never got the chance to say it, because when he turned his head, her lips made direct contact with *his*.

And just like that, an unexpected, harmless kiss on the cheek turned into something else.

It turned into an actual kiss, and what had started out as fleeting evolved into a great deal more.

Surprised, Miranda began to pull back, but then

paused as their contact blossomed into something far more intense than just a kiss between friends.

Before she knew it, Miranda had her arms around his neck and he had his wrapped around her waist, drawing her closer as the kiss deepened.

He was making her breathless, which in turn was making her head spin.

What was going on here?

And how did she get it to continue?

Chapter Eleven

Colin had no idea what came over him. He had never been one of those men who would size up a woman, biding his time until he could seduce her. It wasn't that he was immune to attractive women. He just felt maintaining any sort of a relationship with one was too complicated, and one-night stands could prove to be troublesome.

He found it easier just to steer clear.

But there was something incredibly compelling about this particular woman that just reeled him in. There was no other explanation as to why he'd sought her out tonight when he didn't have to.

And why else was he even considering showing up at that hospital ward of hers? He'd never thought of himself as someone to take up causes or go that extra mile. Yes, he'd been in the Marines, and yes, he'd become a police officer, but neither had come about out of some compulsive need to help his fellow man. He'd joined the Marines and later the police force because it just seemed like the thing to do at the time. The situations suited him; it was as simple as that.

But although Miranda Steele presented herself as straightforward, there was nothing simple about this woman. And right now, he had an uneasy feeling he was in way over his head. Though he wasn't someone who was ruled by desire, Colin had a feeling there would be no turning back for him if he stayed here a minute longer. And he wasn't all that certain that the road ahead was one he should be venturing onto.

The sound of Lola barking in the background was what finally broke apart the moment—and forced him back to his senses.

Taking a step away from her, he looked at Miranda. Her lipstick was blurred from the imprint of his lips and she looked as dazed as he felt.

He was shaken up inside and it was a struggle not to show it. "Did you do that so that I'd come down to your children's ward?"

That hurt, Miranda thought. Did he really believe she was that kind of person? The kind who physically manipulated people?

"No," she answered, her voice low as she tried to collect herself. "I was just trying to kiss your cheek. *You* were the one who turned his head."

His expression remained stoic and unyielding. "So you're not trying to seduce me into seeing things your way?"

"No, I'm not," Miranda cried, stunned. The moment had shattered and what had seemed so wonderful a second ago no longer was. "Forget I asked you," she told him stiffly.

Damn it, those were tears filling her eyes. He hadn't meant for any of that to happen. He wasn't accustomed to dealing with a woman who didn't have some ulterior motive—except for his aunt.

Hell, he wasn't really used to dealing with women at all, Colin thought, feeling helpless and annoyed at the same time.

Unable to find the right words to express his regret for having hurt her, he marched to the front door, opened it and stepped outside.

He heard the door close behind him. Heard the lock being flipped into place. For just a split second, he considered turning around and knocking on the panel, to apologize.

But words didn't come to him now any more than they had before.

If he tried to say anything, he'd only make things worse, he knew. Communication was not his forte, so instead he walked away.

Numb, confused, Miranda wiped away the tears sliding down her cheeks with the back of her hand. She wasn't all that sure what had just happened here. All she knew was that Colin had taken off like a man who had been ambushed and then suddenly given the chance for a clean getaway.

She heard a car starting up and then taking off.

His car.

She didn't understand. He had given off mixed signals. Why had he bothered coming over in the first place?

Turning away from the door, she sighed. "I really do wish I was a mind reader, Colin. Then maybe I could understand what's going on here."

She realized that she was absently running her fingertips along her lips. She could almost swear she could still feel his lips against hers.

Taste his lips against hers.

She closed her eyes for a moment, trying to focus her brain. She'd never been the type to let a guy throw her, or mess with her mind. But she'd never *felt* what she had felt this evening when he'd kissed her.

"C'mon, Miranda, this isn't like you. Get a grip." Opening her eyes, she saw that Lola was looking at her as if she understood what was going on here.

"You're right, Lola. I don't have time to waste like this. We have a tree to decorate and we don't need anybody's help, right, girl?"

Lola yipped, making her laugh.

"Of course right. So let's get started. I'll hang, you supervise. Deal?"

Lola barked again.

"Deal," Miranda agreed, grinning.

With that, she went to the garage to get the ladder she was going to need in order to reach the higher branches.

Colin did his best to talk himself out of it and he succeeded.

For a day.

But the following day, he did something he had never done before. He called in and told his sergeant that he was taking half of one of his many accumulated vacation days.

The man sounded rather surprised. "Just a half day?"

"That's all," Colin answered.

If he took the whole day, he knew he'd wind up getting roped into spending the entire time visiting sick kids—kids who didn't have the odds in their favor. He didn't like admitting that he wasn't strong enough to face something like that for more than a short amount of time.

It was obvious that Miranda was made of stronger stuff than he was, which was why he was going to the oncology ward as she'd wanted him to. He owed her an apology for the way he'd behaved the other night, and this was the only way he knew how to apologize.

He was probably going to regret this, Colin thought, not for the first time. But if nothing else, he was a man who always paid his debts. It was part of his code.

Miranda peered into one of the few private rooms that were located on the floor. Jason Greeley still appeared to be asleep. His mom had been here with the little boy all night. But the single mother had to go to work, so had left an hour ago. Since then Miranda had been checking on the five-year-old every few minutes. She didn't want him waking up by himself.

Moving closer to the boy, she adjusted his covers. "You usually don't sleep this long after a treatment, Jason," she said, deliberately sounding cheerful. Cheer begot cheer, in her opinion. "Don't turn lazy on me now. Your mama was here all night. She hates leaving you, but she had to go to work. But don't worry, she'll be back soon. And I'll be here all day until she gets here," Miranda promised.

The boy stirred a little, but didn't open his eyes. His even breathing told her that he was still sleeping.

Miranda went on talking as if he could hear every word she said. "I've got cherry Jell-O waiting for you the second you open your eyes. You told me that was your favorite, so I made sure there's plenty. All you have to do to get some is open your eyes. C'mon, baby, it's not that hard."

When he didn't, Miranda sighed. "Okay, play hard to get. But you're going to have to open them sometime. No sense in letting all that cherry Jell-O go to waste, you know."

"How do you do it? How do you deal with this without falling apart?"

Startled, pressing one hand against her chest to contain the heart that had all but leaped out, nearly cracking her rib cage, she swung around to see Colin, all 6'2" and broad-shouldered, standing just inside the room. He was wearing his police uniform.

It took her a second to find her voice. "What are you doing here?"

"I was in the neighborhood and thought I'd drop by," he quipped. And then his voice lowered. "Besides, I figured after the other evening, I kind of owed it to you."

She wasn't sure if he was referring to the kiss they'd shared or his walking out on her, but felt it best not to pursue the question. He was here, and right now, that was all that mattered.

"You don't owe me anything," she told him. "But these kids will get a big kick out of seeing a real police officer." And then she glanced at her watch. It was early. "Speaking of which, aren't you supposed to be out there, handing out tickets right now?"

"I took half a vacation day." He expected her to ask him why he hadn't taken a full day, followed by a whole bunch of other questions. Instead she just smiled at him, looking pleased.

"That's great," she enthused. "But if you're only here for a little while, we'll have to make the most of it."

He wasn't sure exactly what she had in mind, but he'd come to expect the unexpected with Miranda. "And exactly how are we going to do that?"

Her mind was already racing. "We've got a big recreation room where the kids play games and where we hold their birthday parties. Right now, it's where we put up the ward's Christmas tree."

"But all the kids aren't—"

She knew what he was going to say—that there were more holidays than just Christmas this season. She answered his question before he had a chance to voice it. "That's all right. All kids like bright lights and presents. It helps to cheer them up a little."

"And feel normal?" he guessed. That had to be what she was shooting for.

"They *are* normal," Miranda told him calmly. She had to make him understand. "They just have more than their share of health issues, but you'd be surprised how they bear up to that. It makes me ashamed when I let everyday, mundane problems overwhelm me."

"You? Overwhelmed?" he asked, teasing her. "I don't believe it. Joan of Arc would probably see you as a role model."

That was his idea of a joke, she realized. Her smile widened.

"Mama?" Jason opened his eyes and looked around the room, disoriented, obviously expecting to see his mother there instead of his nurse and a strange policeman.

"Hey, I didn't mean to wake him up." Colin looked contrite as he addressed Miranda. "I'm sorry," he murmured.

She put her hand on his arm to keep him from leaving. "No, this is a good thing," she assured him. "We were waiting for him to wake up." She turned her attention back to the boy. "Jason, guess what? Remember that police officer I told you about?"

"The one who wouldn't give you a ticket," Jason answered. "I remember."

"That's right, he didn't give me a ticket," she repeated, raising her eyes to Colin's for a moment before shifting them back to the boy. Colin looked surprised. "Well, this is him—and he's here to visit," Miranda announced.

"Cool," the little boy said, with as much enthusiasm as he was able to muster, given that he was still trying to come around. Shifting in his bed, he looked to Miranda for help. "I want to sit up."

Colin was about to press a button on the remote control attached to the guardrail on the boy's bed when he saw Miranda slowly shake her head at him.

"You remember what to do, Jason," she prompted. "We practiced."

"Oh yeah." Small fingers pulled the remote a little closer and then pushed one of the arrows. The back of his bed began to rise. He beamed, looking very proud of himself. "I got it right."

"Of course you did." She tousled his hair affectionately. "That's because you're such a smart boy."

Jason's chocolate brown eyes shifted to look at the policeman who had come to visit him. "Is that a real badge?" he asked, pointing toward Colin's chest.

He glanced down and nodded. "It sure is."

Jason looked at him hopefully. "Is it okay if I touch it?"

Colin came closer and leaned over the boy's bed. "Go ahead."

Small fingers reached out and very slowly and reverently traced the outline of the badge.

"Wow," Jason murmured. "When I grow up, I'm gonna be a police officer just like you."

No one had ever said anything like that to him before—since he didn't interact with children—and Colin found himself truly moved, more than he thought possible. Especially since the boy was talking so positively about a future he might not live to see.

"And you'll be a really great police officer. Maybe even a police detective, if you study very hard," Miranda told the little boy. She could see that Colin had been affected. It wasn't that she wasn't as moved as

Colin. She had just learned to handle her own onslaught of emotions so they wouldn't get in the way of her being the best possible nurse she could be for the sake of the children.

"I'll study *real* hard," Jason promised. He sounded sleepy. And then he yawned. "I'm tired, Miranda."

"Well, then I suggest you'd better get some sleep," she coaxed.

It was obvious that he was trying not to let his eyes close. "But then I'll miss seeing Officer Colin," the boy protested.

"Tell you what," Colin said. "I'll come by again and see you before I leave."

"And will you be back tomorrow, too?" the little boy asked. It was clear that he was losing his battle to keep his eyes open.

"Not tomorrow," Colin answered honestly. "But I'll come back soon."

"Promise?" Jason asked sleepily.

"I promise," Colin told him, saying the words as solemnly as if he were talking to an adult.

But the boy was already asleep again.

Miranda moved the covers up higher on Jason's small body. "That was very nice of you," she told Colin with genuine warmth.

He shrugged. "I didn't do anything out of the ordinary."

"Jason might argue with you about that—if he could argue," she added, looking at the boy with affection. She glanced at her watch. "C'mon, we need to spread that charm of yours around before your coach turns into a pumpkin."

Colin shook his head, mystified. "I never understand half of what you're talking about."

Miranda laughed. "You might just be better off that way."

He inclined his head in agreement. "I was thinking the same thing."

But Miranda didn't hear him. She was on her smartphone, busy summoning the other nurses.

Chapter Twelve

In less than three minutes after Miranda finished making her call, the hallway outside Jason's room was alive with activity.

As Colin looked on in amazement, nurses and orderlies pushed children in wheelchairs and patiently guided others who were using walkers, crutches or braving the way to the recreational room on their own under the watchful eye of an aide or a parent.

To Colin, it looked as if an organized mass evacuation was having a dry run. The whole thing seemed incredible to him, given the average age of the children. However, rather than leaving the building, everyone was going to the large recreation room that currently held the Christmas tree.

Glancing back, Miranda realized that the "guest of honor" directly responsible for this mass migration was still standing just outside Jason's doorway. Determined to change that, she took Colin's hand in hers.

"C'mon," she coaxed.

The expression on his face was rather uncertain as he took in the masses. "That's an awful lot of kids," he told her.

She gently tugged on his hand. "They don't bite," she said cheerfully. "And having them all together in one place means you won't have to repeat yourself. You can say things just once."

The uncertain expression deepened. "What things?"

Miranda had nothing specific to offer, but she was confident that issue would be resolved naturally.

"It'll come to you," she promised. "And the kids'll probably drown you in questions once they get started. C'mon," she coaxed again, drawing him down the hallway. "You're not afraid of a bunch of little kids."

She said it as if she believed it, Colin thought. And it wasn't the kids he was afraid of; he was afraid of inadvertently saying something that might wind up hurting one of them.

But now that she had started this parade of hospitalized children, like some sort of modern-day Pied Piper, he couldn't very well hang back and watch from the sidelines. The sidelines had virtually disappeared in any case, as Colin found himself surrounded on all sides by children streaming into the rec room.

"Kids," Miranda said in a slightly louder voice, when the commotion had died down and the children had all settled in. "This is my friend Officer Kirby. When I told him that some of you had never met a policeman or seen one up close before, he insisted on coming by to say hello." Turning to look at Colin over her shoulder, she grinned at him and said, "Say hello, Officer Kirby."

On the spot and feeling decidedly awkward, Colin murmured, "Hello."

The moment he did, a cacophony of "Hellos," mostly out of sync, echoed back at him.

Pattie, a little girl with curly red hair seated in a wheelchair in the front row, was the first to speak up. "Are you really a policeman?" she asked.

"Yes." And then, doing his best not to sound so wooden, Colin added, "I am."

The two extra words seemed to open up the floodgates. Suddenly he heard questions coming at him from all directions.

"Do you have a gun?" one boy in the back asked.

"Do you shoot people?" a boy beside him added.

"How many bad guys have you caught?" a little blonde girl ventured, while a smaller girl with almost violet eyes shyly asked him if he was "a good cop."

Taking pity on him, Miranda spoke up, hoping that the piece of information she told them would somehow help the children to get a better image of the kind of police work he did. "Officer Kirby rides a motorcycle."

A dark-haired boy with crutches beside his chair cried, "Cool!"

A little girl to Colin's left asked, "Can you do a wheelie?"

"Did you ever fall off your motorcycle?" one little boy wearing a brace asked. "I fell off my bicycle once and broke my neck bone."

"Your collarbone," Miranda corrected gently.

"Oh yeah, my collarbone," he amended. He was still waiting for an answer. "Did you ever fall off?" he asked again.

"No," Colin answered. "I never have."

"Did it take you a long time to learn how to ride your motorcycle?" a little girl sitting near the Christmas tree asked.

As he began fielding the questions a little more comfortably, more and more came his way. Before he knew it, Colin found himself immersed in a give-and-take dialogue with approximately twenty-five children of varying ages, confined to the hospital ward for a number of different reasons.

He was surprised, given the relative seriousness of their conditions, how eager the children all seemed to hear about his job and what he did on his patrols.

Some asked run-of-the-mill questions, like how long it had taken him to become a police officer. Others wanted to know what he thought about while he was out on patrol. Still others asked totally unrelated questions.

The queries came one after another, some voiced eagerly, others shyly, but there were no awkward silences. Everyone had questions, usually more than one. Or two.

Pleased, Miranda stood back, happy to see the children so caught up in their visitor. She kept a watchful eye on Colin, as well, ready to step in if it got to be too much for him. But as the minutes went by, she was fairly certain that he was doing fine. He didn't need her to bail him out.

When the motorcycle officer answered a little girl

named Shelly's question if he'd ever had a pet hamster—
he hadn't—Miranda finally decided he'd had enough
for one day and stepped in.

"I'm afraid Officer Kirby is going to have to be
going," she told the children. The news was met with
youthful voices melding in a mournful "Oh," tinged
with surprise as well as disappointment.

"Can he come back?" the girl with the curly red hair,
Pattie, asked. Then, not waiting for Miranda to reply,
she took her question straight to the horse's mouth. "Can
you, Officer Kirby?"

"If I get the chance," Colin answered diplomatically.

Progress, Miranda thought. She'd expected him to
make an excuse outright. The fact that he hadn't, that
he'd said something half hopeful in response, made her
feel that he was beginning to come around and see the
light.

He was starting to see the children as people.

"When?" A persistent little boy wearing a wool cap
over his bare head looked at his new hero hopefully.

"When his sergeant can spare him again," Miranda
told the child, grasping at the first handy excuse that
came to her. The look in Colin's eyes when their glances
met assured her she'd come up with a good one. "Now,
everybody, say goodbye to Officer Kirby."

A swell of voices, more enthusiastic since the kids
had gotten to spend some time with him, chorused
loudly, "Goodbye, Officer Kirby," while others added,
"Come back soon!"

Putting her hand on Colin's elbow, Miranda took
control of the situation. She gently guided him out of

the room. They swung by Jason's room and he spent a little time there.

After that, Miranda walked him to the elevators.

"Well, you survived," she observed happily, offering him a pleased smile.

"I guess I did, didn't I?" There was no missing the relief, as well as the surprise, in his voice. Colin paused, looking back over his shoulder in the general direction of the rec room. "Are all those kids…you know…?"

Somehow, even though he'd spent more than an hour talking with them, Colin couldn't get himself to say the word. Saying it made it that much more of an evil reality.

Miranda seemed to know exactly what he was trying to ask her. If the children were terminal.

"Treatments have greatly improved over the last five years. A lot of those kids have more of a fighting chance to beat the odds and get well, or at least have their diseases go into remission. Meanwhile, every day they have is special to them, and we all have to make the most of it.

"They really enjoyed having you come," Miranda went on. "Thank you for letting me bully you into coming to the hospital to talk to them."

"Is that what you call it?" he asked, amusement curving his mouth. "Bullying?"

"No," she admitted honestly, raising her eyes to his. "I don't. But that's what I figure you'd call it, so I thought I'd put it into terms that you could relate to more easily."

Her eyes were at it again, he thought. Doing that funny little laughing, twinkly thing that captivated him.

The elevator arrived and he put his hand against one of the doors to keep it from closing. He searched for words to answer her and finally said, "Maybe I'll let you bully me into it again soon."

There was no other way to describe it but to say that he saw joy leap into her face. "Just say the word," she told him.

Doing his best not to stare, Colin nodded. "Maybe I will," he said.

Stepping inside the elevator, he dropped his hand. Her smile was the last thing he saw before the doors shut.

During the remainder of the day, after he returned to the precinct and went on duty, Colin tried to tell himself that the heat he was experiencing radiating through his chest and his gut was nothing more than a case of heartburn. But he had a strong suspicion that even if he consumed an entire bottle of antacid tablets, that wouldn't have any effect on the warmth that was pervading him.

He should have been annoyed. That pushy woman had invaded his world and messed with his routine. She'd completely messed up the natural order of things.

But somehow, try as he might, he couldn't drum up the slightest bit of irritation. To make matters worse, he caught himself thinking about her.

A lot.

Thinking about her and wondering if he wasn't inadvertently sealing his own doom if he just happened to stop by her place and see her again sometime in the near future.

Like tonight.

Telling himself that it was the holiday season and that everyone was guilty of experiencing some sort of generosity of spirit—why try to be different?—he didn't go home after his shift was over. Instead, he hung around the precinct for a while, killing time by catching up on the paperwork that was the bane of every police officer's existence.

And when he was finished and he'd made sure to file all the reports before leaving, Colin decided to play the odds. For this to work out, Miranda needed to be home instead of one of the two places she volunteered.

He had less than a fifty-fifty chance of finding her there, but he went and picked up a pizza anyway.

With the tantalizing aroma from the pizza box filling the interior of his vehicle, Colin made one more quick stop, at a pet store that was along the way, and then drove on to his final destination, Miranda's house.

He wasn't aware of holding his breath that last half mile until he found himself releasing it.

Her car was parked in the driveway.

Apparently, Miranda was done doing good deeds for the day, Colin thought happily as he parked his vehicle at the curb and got out.

When he passed her car on the way to her front door, he felt heat coming from her engine.

She must have gotten home just minutes ago, he thought with a faint smile.

Juggling the extra-large pizza, Colin rang the doorbell. Inside, Lola instantly began barking. The familiar sound was oddly comforting, though he couldn't begin to explain why. He was afraid that if he thought about it too much, he'd turn right around and go home. Coming here like this carried many implications, and he wasn't sure he was ready to face them.

The best way to deal with those implications at the moment was just to ignore them. Ignore them and focus on the hungry feeling in the pit of his stomach. The one that involved not having eaten.

When Miranda opened the door she was obviously more than a little surprised to see him.

"Hi, what's up?"

"Um, I thought that since you made me dinner that other time, I should reciprocate." Rather than continue—because he felt himself about to trip over his tongue—he held up the cardboard box. "Pizza," he added needlessly, since the aroma—as well as the shape and the label—clearly gave away what he had brought.

"You made me a pizza?" Miranda asked, amused.

Her question threw him for a second. "What? No. I picked this up on the way over here. I guarantee you wouldn't want to eat any pizza that I made," he told her with a self-deprecating laugh.

"Oh, it couldn't be all that bad," she stated, ushering Colin in and then closing the door behind him.

Lola came bounding over the moment he walked in. The animal's attention was totally focused on him and, more specifically, the aromatic box he was carrying.

Miranda caught the dog's collar to keep the German shepherd from knocking Colin over. "She's happy to see you."

Colin harbored no such illusions. "She smells the pizza," he said.

"And you," Miranda added. "Dogs have incredibly keen senses of smell—and they can separate one thing from another. The pizza's the draw," she agreed. "But Lola clearly *likes* you."

Colin made no acknowledgment of that statement one way or the other. Instead, he took a small paper bag out of his jacket pocket. The sack had the insignia of a local pet store chain embossed on it. Thinking ahead, he had stopped to pick up several doggie treats before coming by. At the very least, he'd wanted to be able to distract the dog for a few minutes so that he and Miranda could have their pizza in peace.

"I brought these for her," he announced, passing the bag of treats to Miranda.

Opening it, she looked inside and then smiled broadly at him.

"I think that before the evening is over, Lola is going to be madly in love with you."

Lola had begun to nudge the paper bag with her nose before Miranda finished her sentence.

"I was just hoping to distract her long enough for us to eat the pizza," Colin explained.

Miranda laughed. "In that case, you should have bought out the entire pet shop. Have you ever watched a dog eat? It's like watching a furry vacuum cleaner. The treats'll be gone before we have a chance to sit down.

"But that's okay," she assured Colin. "I've been

working with her and she's getting to be a little more well behaved than she was." Her grin widened as she added, "We might even get to eat an entire slice apiece before she starts begging for a bite—or ten. The trick," Miranda told him with a wink, "is not to give in."

Easier said than done, Colin thought. The dog was already looking up at her with soulful eyes.

Chapter Thirteen

"I see you finished decorating your Christmas tree," Colin commented as he followed her into the kitchen.

Miranda nodded cheerfully. "Yes, finally. All those boxes and ornaments were starting to make the living room a real obstacle course, not to mention pretty messy. So I made up my mind that I wasn't going to go to bed until I had hung the last ornament on the tree.

"The next day I happily put all the boxes away." She looked down at the dog, who was eyeing the pizza box as if expecting to see slices come leaping out. "This way Lola has a little more room to move around, don't you, girl?"

"She doesn't strike me as the type to be put off by a bunch of boxes," he observed. "I can see her plowing through them."

"She kind of does plow through things when she wants to get somewhere," Miranda agreed.

He set down the pizza box and watched her take a couple plates from the cupboard. She placed them on either side of the box. "I thought you said she was becoming more obedient."

"I said we were *working* on it," she corrected. "Right now," Miranda told him, patting the German shepherd's head, "she's a work in progress."

There was no missing the affection in the woman's voice. "You seem kind of attached to her," Colin observed.

"It's hard not to be." Taking out a bottle of beer, she set it next to Colin's plate. "She's very affectionate and lovable." She saw the confused way Colin was looking at the beer. "I just replaced the can you drank the other day," she explained.

"Uh-huh," he responded, taking her explanation at face value. He waited for her to sit down opposite him. "What are you going to do when someone adopts her?" he asked.

"Be happy for her," she answered.

Her response sounded rather automatic to him. Miranda probably meant that on some level, because she was a selfless person. But on another level, he had a feeling she would miss the German shepherd a great deal if the dog was placed in another home. "Why don't you adopt her?"

Taking a large slice of pizza, she bit into it. And then laughed softly. "If I adopted every dog I fostered, I'd wind up being cited by the police for having way too many dogs in my house. This area isn't zoned for kennels," she reminded him.

He shrugged. After all, she probably knew what was best for her. It was just that there seemed to be a bond between her and the dog she was fostering. But then, he hadn't known Miranda all that long and most likely she was like this with all the dogs she took care of— just like she was with all the children she looked after at the hospital.

"This is really good pizza," she commented. Looking at the box, she read the name written across the top. "Rizzoli's." She shook her head. It didn't ring a bell. I don't think I'm familiar with that chain."

"That's because it's not a chain," he told her. He was finishing up his second slice and then slid a third one onto his plate in between washing them down with beer. "It's this little hole-in-the-wall of a place in the next town. Easy to miss," he told her. "It's been there for about twenty years. I discovered it when I moved back to Bedford."

"The next town?" Miranda repeated. "That's a long way to travel for something that's available in practically every shopping center in Bedford."

Colin shrugged and then his eyes met hers. "Sometimes quality is worth going the extra mile or so."

Miranda grinned. Leaning over, she took her napkin and wiped away a dab of sauce from the corner of his mouth. Maybe it was her imagination, but she could have sworn a spark of electricity zapped through her. "I'm glad you think so."

What was she up to? he wondered, and why was he

so captivated by her? Why wasn't he just walking out instead of sitting here across from this do-gooder?

"Why do I feel like I'm being set up for something?" he asked Miranda.

"Because you're a cop and you're naturally suspicious," she replied with a warm laugh. "You're not being set up for anything," she told him, and heaven help him, he believed her. "Besides, setting you up would be an awful way to pay you back for bringing over this really great pizza."

Lola had been whimpering since they'd started eating. Her whimper was growing louder by increments. Obviously antsy, the German shepherd had moved from Miranda's right side to her left and then back again, watching her with big brown eyes that seemed to grow larger each time she moved.

Upping her game, Lola dipped her head and slipped it under Miranda's arm, nudging it.

Miranda laughed. "Okay, okay, I surrender." Tearing off a piece from her slice, she held it out to the dog. Less than half a second later, the piece was gone, disappearing between Lola's teeth.

"Hey, you could lose a finger that way," Colin warned, instantly alert.

"No, she's very careful," she assured him. "For a dog with such big teeth, Lola's incredibly gentle when she takes food from my hand."

He knew that in Miranda's place, he would have flinched, hearing those teeth click shut. But she had remained completely unfazed. "I take it this isn't the first time she's eaten out of your hand."

"No, it's not," she confirmed. "Lola likes to kibitz when I'm having dinner."

"You're spoiling her," he told her. There was disapproval in his voice.

It was Miranda's turn to shrug. "Lola's been through so much, I figure she's entitled to a little spoiling." As he watched, Miranda's expression darkened. "Her last owner chained her up in the backyard, then beat her and starved her. He didn't give her any water, either."

"How did Lola wind up at the shelter?" Colin asked her.

"A neighbor heard her whimpering and looked over this guy's fence. Lola was half-dead. Horrified, he called the police. They arrived just in time. Another couple of days and Lola would have died," she told him fiercely. "Needless to say, they took her away."

Colin had set his beer down when she started telling him about Lola's background. "What happened to the owner?" he asked.

Every time she thought about the incident, Miranda was filled with anger.

"He got off with a fine. If it were up to me, I would have had him drawn and quartered in the town square and made an example of." She saw Colin looking at her incredulously. She wondered if she'd set off some alarms in his head since, after all, the man was a police officer. "What?"

"I've just never seen you angry before. I didn't think you were capable of it," he confessed.

"Oh, I'm capable of it all right," Miranda assured him. "Cruelty of any kind gets me very angry—especially when it comes to children or animals." She saw his re-action. "Why are you grinning?"

For once his poker face failed him. "You look kind of…I don't know…*cute* when you get angry like that. You don't exactly fit the part of an avenging angel, that's all."

Miranda pressed her lips together, but her anger was abating. Her eyes did narrow a little, though. "You're making fun of me," she accused.

"No, not really." He polished off yet another pizza slice. "It's just nice to know that you have this darker side to you. Up until now," he admitted, "I wasn't sure you were human."

"I'm all too human," Miranda told him. She pushed away her plate. "I'm also stuffed."

Colin doubted it. "You only had two and a half slices," he pointed out.

"And I'm stuffed," Miranda repeated.

"How?" he asked. He nodded at the dog, who was still circling the table. "Lola could probably eat more than you just did."

"Undoubtedly," Miranda agreed with a laugh. She watched the dog for a moment "She burns it all up run-ning around in the backyard."

Colin snorted. "And you, of course, just lie around like a slug."

Tickled, Miranda grinned at his assessment. "I don't need much fuel."

He nodded at her empty plate. "Obviously."

Her attention shifted toward the open pizza box. There were several slices still in it. "Speaking of which, why don't you take what's left home with you when you go? You can do it more justice than I would. And if you leave it here, I'll only wind up giving it to Lola when she starts begging."

He sighed, shaking his head. "You're going to have to learn how to say no."

Amusement curved her mouth as she raised her eyes to his. "I'm working on it."

For just a moment, he wondered if Miranda was putting him on some kind of notice—and if she felt she needed to. Which in turn led him to wonder why. Was she afraid that he thought bringing over pizza entitled him to make a move on her?

Where the hell had that come from? Colin silently demanded. He was here because he was paying her back for the dinner she'd made him, nothing more. He certainly wasn't thinking of her in any sort of a romantic light. Just because they'd accidentally kissed didn't mean he wanted to capitalize on it—even if it *had* been a memorable kiss.

Damn it, he upbraided himself, he was overthinking the whole thing. Maybe he *should* go home now.

As he wrestled with his thoughts, Miranda rose and took her plate to the sink.

He still had part of a slice—his fifth one—on his plate. Making a decision, Colin picked up what was left of it and lowered his hand to Lola's level.

On cue, the German shepherd quickly rounded the table to his side. Colin hardly saw her open her mouth. Just like that, the pizza was gone.

"Now who's spoiling her?" Miranda asked with a knowing laugh.

Colin's shoulders rose and fell in a careless shrug. "I don't like seeing food go to waste," he told her.

"Neither do I," she replied. "Of course, if I keep this up with Lola, she is definitely going to wind up being a blimp."

He looked at the dog, who seemed to know that no more slices were coming her way tonight. With a satisfied yawn, she stretched out at his feet.

This was far too domestic a scene, Colin thought uneasily. He really should be on his way home.

But somehow, he remained sitting where he was. "I don't think there's much chance of that," he told Miranda. "She looks pretty lean to me."

"Hear that, Lola?" Miranda asked. She finished drying her hands and left the towel hanging on the hook next to the refrigerator. "The nice police officer just paid you a compliment."

Hearing her name, Lola barked in response.

Miranda's eyes crinkled as she suppressed a laugh. "She says thank you," she told Colin.

"You didn't tell me you can communicate with dogs." But to be honest, it wouldn't have surprised him if she said she did.

"You don't have to speak the language to be able to communicate," Miranda answered. Rather than sit down at the table again, she paused and glanced toward the rear of the house. "Oh, by the way, I have something for you."

"What do you mean by 'something'?" he asked warily, on his guard.

"Don't look so worried. It's not a bribe," Miranda teased. "It's harmless. Wait right here." With that, she hurried out of the kitchen. "I got it on my lunch break," she called, raising her voice so that it carried back to him.

Minutes later, Miranda returned to the kitchen, carrying a two-foot potted fir tree. The tree was decorated with a string of lights and tiny silver and blue Christmas balls.

"This is for you," she told him, setting the tree on the table. "I took a chance that you still hadn't gotten a Christmas tree."

"I didn't," he answered.

Colin was about to add that he had no plans to get one and that he *never* got a tree at Christmas time. The last time there'd been a Christmas tree in his house, he was living at his aunt's and the tree in question had been hers, not his.

But something stopped him from telling Miranda any of that, at least for now.

"I was going to get a bigger tree, but I didn't think you'd want it, so I settled for this small, live one," she explained.

He didn't want one at all, but since she'd gone to the trouble of going out and buying it for him, he bit his tongue and refrained from saying that.

Instead, curious, he asked her, "Did the tree come with decorations?"

"Not exactly," she confessed. "But to be honest, I

didn't think you'd decorate it if I handed you a naked tree, so I did it for you. It was kind of fun, being able to deck out a Christmas tree in half an hour." Her momentum picked up as she added, "And when the season's over, you can plant it in your backyard."

"Just one problem with that," Colin told her. He broke off a small piece from one of the remaining pizza slices. Out of the corner of his eye, he saw Lola come to attention again. "I don't have a backyard."

Miranda never missed a beat. "Or you can transplant it into a larger pot as it starts to get bigger." Second-guessing Colin's objection to that suggestion, she offered, "I could do that for you if you're too busy."

"Because you have so much time on your hands," he said with a touch of sarcasm. He felt his conscience taking him to task. Miranda was only trying to be nice, he reminded himself. "Sorry, I didn't mean that the way it came out."

"No offense taken," she told him. "Besides, haven't you ever heard the old saying 'If you want something done, ask a busy person to do it'?"

"No, I haven't. But I'll take your word for it." He looked at the tree with its dainty ornaments and the bright red foil wrapped around its base. "Thanks. It's a nice-looking tree." He left it standing on the table for now. "But you really didn't have to get me one," Colin stressed.

"Let's just say it makes me happy doing so," she told him. "I couldn't stand the idea of you not having at least a little tree—so I got you one."

It was little, but he would have preferred an even smaller one—or better yet, none at all.

Colin pinned her with a piercing look. "But why would that bother you?" he couldn't help asking. "Not having a tree doesn't bother me."

"I know, but it does me." She could see they could go on dancing endlessly around the same point, so she tried something else. "It's a reminder of goodwill toward one another."

It took a lot to suppress the laugh that rose to his lips, but somehow, he managed. "Maybe if everyone thought the way you do, there'd be no need to be reminded. It would just be a given," Colin mused.

"That's the nicest thing anyone ever said to me," she told him, her eyes misting.

"If it's so nice, why are you crying?" he asked. If he lived to be a hundred and fifty, he would never understand women.

Miranda shrugged. "I guess I'm one of those people who cries when she's happy."

Colin shook his head. "Talk about mixed signals," he murmured.

He needed to leave.

He could feel barriers weakening within him, walls being breached and beliefs he'd held as hard and fast truths dissolving like cotton candy left out in the rain.

This woman was turning him inside out without lifting a finger, he thought grudgingly. If he didn't leave now, he didn't know what sort of mental condition he'd be in by the time he *did* leave.

"Okay," he said, rising. "I'd better be going." Belatedly, he remembered the little Christmas tree on the table. "Thanks for the tree."

"Thank *you* for dinner and for coming to the hospital today," she told him. "The kids just couldn't stop talking about you after you left. You were definitely the highlight of their week."

He had no idea how to respond to that. Being on the receiving end of gratitude was totally new to him. "Yeah, no problem."

"Oh, I think it was a problem for you, which was why having you come was so special—for everyone," she added meaningfully.

"You included?"

Now why the hell had he just said that? Was he *asking* for trouble? Colin silently demanded.

Miranda took a breath before answering. "Me most of all."

Chapter Fourteen

The moment, wrapped in silence, stretched out for a long time. He didn't know how to respond to what she'd just said.

Me most of all.

Finally, he stumbled through an awkward answer. "Oh, um, good to know."

Miranda felt sorry for him. Colin looked completely out of his element. Deftly, she changed the direction of the conversation.

"I'll walk you to your car," she offered.

"No," he said, perhaps a little too forcefully. All he wanted to do now was to get into his vehicle—quickly—and drive away. "You don't have to," he added.

She nodded at the things still on the table. "You can't carry the Christmas tree and the pizza box at the same time."

The German shepherd presented herself right next to him, a plaintive look on her face. He read between the lines.

"Um, I think that Lola would probably prefer if I left the pizza here."

Miranda pushed the pizza along the table so it was closer to him.

"Which is exactly why you're taking it with you. Too much people food isn't good for her and you've already seen what a pushover I am around Lola."

He wasn't accustomed to women who owned their shortcomings. He found himself smiling at Miranda in acknowledgment. "That's something you're going to have to overcome when you have kids."

He'd just said *when*, not *if*, Miranda noted. Was that just a careless slip of the tongue on his part, or did Colin really see her as a mother?

She rather liked the idea that he did. Of course, that would have to mean she'd have to slow down long enough to actually *have* a child.

Miranda took the pizza box, leaving the Christmas tree for him to carry. When he picked it up, they began to walk to the front door.

"Disciplining is something that I think I'll delegate to my husband," she told him, adding, "He'll probably be the strong and masterful type."

Colin's laugh was dry as he thought over her comment. "He would have to be."

Miranda cocked her head, trying to decide how he meant that. "Was that a compliment or a criticism?" she asked, curious.

He was talking too much, Colin decided. That had never been a problem for him before he'd met this woman.

"Take it any way you want," he answered, thinking that being vague was the safest way to go right now.

Miranda felt Lola trying to crowd her, attempting to push her way outside.

"No, girl, you have to stay in. I'll be right back," she promised.

Tucking the pizza box under her arm, she cringed slightly as she both heard and felt the remaining slices sliding together.

With her free hand, she gently steered the dog back into the house. Then, trying not to drop the box, she pulled the door closed behind her.

Looking on, Colin said with approval, "You're making progress."

"Well, I had to," Miranda told him. "You were watching me."

"So if I wasn't here…?" He left the end of the sentence up in the air and waited for her to finish it.

She did, but not as he expected. "…I wouldn't have pizza to keep away from her in the first place."

Colin shook his head, impressed despite himself. "I've got to say, you really do know how to dance around a subject."

"I've learned from the best," she said, grinning. She watched his brow furrow as he looked at her over his shoulder, perplexed.

Miranda hadn't meant for it to sound cryptic. Following him to his vehicle, she explained, "Kids. They can spin tales that'll make you dizzy."

Stopping beside his car, Colin looked at her pointedly. "I know the feeling."

He took his keys out of his pocket. Unlocking the doors, he put the potted Christmas tree on the floor in the rear. Taking the pizza, he placed the box on the passenger seat, then turned to face her.

"Well, thanks for your help with the pizza. And thanks for the tree," he added belatedly.

He watched as a smile filled her eyes. "Don't mention it. It's the least I can do after all that joy you brought my kids."

Her thanks made him feel awkward again. "I just showed up," he insisted again, not wanting to make any more out of it than that. But with Miranda he should have known better.

"You did a lot more than that," she insisted. "You brightened up their day. Their parents come as often as they can—and that's a good thing," she assured him. "But having you come to their ward was something out of the ordinary. Something special," she said with feeling.

He opened his mouth and then shut it again. When he saw the curious look on her face, he told her, "Well, I'm not going to argue with you, because I'm beginning to get the feeling that no one stands a chance of winning an argument with you."

"Sure they do," she declared, although, offhand, she couldn't think of a single example to cite.

"Uh-huh." His response as he started to go reeked of skepticism.

"Oh, and Colin?" Miranda called after him, raising her voice.

Colin was about to round the hood to get into his side of the vehicle, but stopped. "Yes?"

"Promise you won't forget and leave the tree in the car. It's a hardy little thing, but if you leave it in the car indefinitely, it'll wilt and lose all its needles."

Indulging her, he promised, "I won't forget."

"Oh, and drive carefully," she called after him.

Colin paused again. He should feel annoyed or insulted that, given the nature of his work, she still felt the need to say something like that to him. And yet this whole scene just made him smile. He had no idea why.

Waiting, he turned around. "Anything else?"

Miranda knew that she was pushing her luck to the absolute limit, but then nothing ventured, nothing gained, right?

Taking a breath, she forged ahead. "Well, there's a Christmas Eve party, if you'd like to come."

He hadn't expected her to say that; he'd just assumed she'd have more trivial slogans to send his way. "At the hospital?"

He'd done his part at the hospital and she was now focusing on the other two places where she volunteered her time.

"Well, yes, there, too," she allowed. "But I was thinking of the shelter."

She still wasn't narrowing it down, he realized. "Homeless or animal?"

"Homeless. Although, now that I think about it, we are having a party at the animal shelter, too," she told him. "It's an adoption party. There's one every month, but there's an extra push to find the animals a home just before Christmas."

"Of course there is." Listening to her, he shook his head. It was a wonder the woman didn't just fall over and collapse. "When do you have time for *you*?" he asked.

"All of this is for me," she responded. Seeing the doubtful look on his face, she insisted, "I derive pleasure out of seeing the animals find new homes and the kids getting better and going back to their families. And the women at the shelter taking stock of their situation and finding a way to create new lives for themselves and their children."

Saints have less to do, he thought. Colin shook his head again, but the corners of his mouth had curved ever so slightly.

"All of this is for you, huh?" He watched as she nodded with feeling. "I don't think I've ever met anyone like you before, Miranda Steele," he told her in all sincerity.

"Is that a good thing?" she asked.

"I'm thinking on it," he answered, remaining deliberately vague.

She couldn't read his expression, and her curiosity was getting the better of her even though she knew it shouldn't. "Let me know what you come up with."

"I have a feeling you'll be the first to know."

Colin suddenly found himself fighting the urge to pull her into his arms. If he didn't leave now, he might wind up doing something stupid, and as unique as this woman was, he didn't need any complications in his life.

He'd already gotten too involved with her as it was.

He needed distance, not closeness, Colin insisted silently.

So why wasn't he getting into his car and leaving? Why was he turning around and crossing back toward the woman?

Miranda was standing at the curb, ready to wave at him as he pulled away.

When instead of leaving, he approached, she looked at him uncertainly, slightly confused even while she felt her heart climbing up into her throat.

Her breath was backing up in her chest. "Did you forget something?"

"Yeah," he muttered. "My sanity."

Her confusion mounted. "I don't know what that means."

Colin didn't respond. At least not verbally. Instead, he took her into his arms just the way he'd told himself not to, and kissed her the way he *knew* he shouldn't.

The way every fiber of his being felt that he just *had* to.

Confusion ran rampant all through Miranda. One moment she was standing at the curb, getting ready to watch Colin drive down the street and disappear; the next moment she found herself smack in the middle of an old-fashioned twister, being sucked up into its very core and whirling around so hard she couldn't breathe. She certainly couldn't think or get her bearings.

But then, bearings were highly overrated, she decided.

Standing up on her toes, Miranda dug her fingertips into his shoulders in a desperate attempt to anchor herself to something solid before she was swept so completely away she would never be able to find her way back again.

This *wasn't* a kiss. She'd been kissed before, kissed by faceless, unremarkable men who faded from her memory before they had a chance to even walk out the door.

But this—*this* was an experience. A mind-blowing, incredible experience that she would remember to her dying day even if she lived to be a hundred and ten.

Colin fought the urge to deepen this kiss and take it to its natural conclusion. Fought the urge to sweep her up into his arms and carry her back inside her house so that he could make love with her. Make love with her until they were both too exhausted to even breathe.

He came within a hair's breadth of giving in to that urge, that desire.

And then a last sliver of sanity rose up, stopping him.

He couldn't do this, he silently insisted, couldn't make love with her. Because if he did, he would be willfully bringing his darkness into her world.

She was a bright, shining ray of light, bent on bringing happiness to everyone and everything. If he took this to its natural conclusion, he would be guilty of if not extinguishing that light, then at the very least dimming it considerably.

He couldn't be responsible for that, couldn't do that to her and all the other lives that Miranda would wind up touching.

Although every fiber of his being fought it, trying to keep him from following through, he separated himself from Miranda. He removed her arms, which she'd wound around his neck, and pushed them down against her sides, held them there for a long moment—until he could collect himself.

"I've got to go," he told her hoarsely.

Then, without another word, Colin got into his car and turned on the ignition. He pulled away from the curb without a single backward glance.

Then, unable to help himself, he looked in the rear-view mirror.

Miranda was still standing there at the curb where he had left her.

A pang of regret seized his very being.

Colin struggled with the impulse to turn the car around and head back to her. Instead, he pushed down hard on the accelerator, determined to put more and more distance between them.

"Count yourself lucky," he said, addressing the figure that was growing progressively smaller and smaller in his rearview mirror. "You don't need someone like me in your life."

He had a very strong feeling that if he had given in to himself tonight, if he had weakened and made love to Miranda, he wouldn't have been able to walk away from her, short of being sandblasted away.

That would be a very bad thing.

For her.

Miranda had a sinking feeling as she watched Colin drive off that he could very well be gone from her life for good.

There'd been something about the set of his shoulders, about the foreboding expression on his face as he had removed her arms from around his neck and stepped away, that made her think of an iron gate coming down, separating the two of them.

Cutting her off from him.

But even so, she kept watching for him every time she looked up, every time her attention was drawn to something—a noise, a flash of light out of the corner of her eye.

Every time she raised her eyes, she was looking for Colin.

And every time she did, he wasn't there.

He wasn't leaning in the doorway of any of the hospital rooms belonging to the small patients she attended, wasn't standing across the street from the animal shelter, waiting for her to come out. He wasn't walking into the women's shelter, wasn't ringing her doorbell and standing on the front step until she opened the door.

He wasn't anywhere in her life—except in her mind, and there he had set up housekeeping, big-time.

If she was going to function properly, she was either going to have to purge him from her mind and forget all about him, or else beard the lion in his den, Miranda thought in a moment of madness.

Get hold of yourself, she silently lectured.

She was far too busy for this, far too busy to mentally dwell on a man who—a man who...

In the middle of her rounds, Miranda abruptly came to a dead stop. She'd initially been drawn to the tall, dark, silent police officer not because he could kiss like nobody's business and set her soul on fire. She'd been drawn to him because of the sadness she saw in his eyes. She remembered thinking that Colin needed someone to brighten his world, to help him find hope and hang on to it.

He needed *her*, and somehow, she had lost sight of that.

But not anymore, she vowed. She was back on track and determined to strip that sadness, that darkness out of him until Officer Colin Kirby found a reason to smile of his own accord.

He could keep those lips to himself. That wasn't what was important here. What she wanted was his happiness.

And she was determined to help him find it if it was the last thing she did.

Chapter Fifteen

Despite his resolve, he couldn't seem to get Miranda out of his head. Not that day, nor the next. The harder he tried, the less success he had. His thoughts turned to the bubbly nurse over a dozen times a day. More, if he was being honest with himself.

For the first time in his adult life, Colin's laser-like focus completely failed him.

He couldn't get himself to concentrate exclusively on his work. Images of Miranda's face kept materializing in his mind's eye at the worst possible times, impeding him at every turn.

Colin had never been one to throw in the towel. He struggled to regain control over himself and his thoughts. He'd triumphed over the racking pain of losing his parents—especially his mother, who he'd been so close to—and managed to keep going during his tour overseas when more than half his platoon had been wiped out all around him.

And though they hadn't been close, guilt had skewered him when he'd lost his partner, Andrew Owens, while on the job.

But he'd managed to rise above all that, erasing it from his mind and functioning as if his insides hadn't been smashed into a thousand pieces. He did it to survive, to continue putting one foot in front of the other and moving on the path he found himself on.

But this—this was completely different. For some mysterious reason, he'd lost his ability to isolate himself, to strip all distracting thoughts from his mind.

He'd lost the ability to continue, and he knew he had to resolve this if he had any hopes of functioning and moving on with his life.

He just had to figure out how.

How had this happened? It felt as if Thanksgiving had been only yesterday, then somehow she'd blinked, and now Christmas was a week away and Miranda had more than enough to keep not just herself but half a dozen people busy.

To paraphrase Dickens, it was both the best time of the year and the worst time of the year, mainly because of all the things that were associated with the season. The shelters as well as the hospital needed her more than ever, and there was enough for her to do thirty-six hours a day if she could somehow find a way to create that many hours out of thin air.

But even with everything she had to handle, she

couldn't stop thinking about Colin. Worrying about Colin. It was interfering not just with her ability to devote herself to her work as a nurse, but also as a volunteer—in both areas that used her services.

She needed to talk to Colin, she decided, and she needed to do it face-to-face, not over the phone. Any other means would be far too impersonal.

Because of the hectic pace this time of year generated, taking time off from the hospital was not an option. The only thing she could do was try to shave a little time from her volunteer work. The pace there was hectic, as well, and there were a great many demands on her time whenever she had any to spare. But she *had* to do this. Because not talking to Colin was unthinkable.

The problem was, since she still didn't know where the man lived, the only place she could hope to find him was along the route he patrolled or at the precinct before he went off duty.

However, both conflicted with her shift at the hospital.

Still, maybe if she played the odds and really hurried— and hopefully he was getting off late—she might be able to catch Colin before he left work for the day.

Miranda felt stressed because even if she was lucky enough to catch him, she'd have to talk fast because the women's shelter's Christmas party, the one she'd helped organize for the children, was scheduled to begin the minute she walked through the door.

She was exhausted already.

As Miranda dashed to her car, all set to take off for the precinct, her cell phone rang.

Please let it be a wrong number, she prayed as she took it out of her purse and then quickly put in her password.

The caller ID that came up belonged to the homeless shelter. Specifically, to Amelia.

Maybe the director was just checking in with her, Miranda thought, mentally crossing her fingers as she answered.

"Hi, Amelia." She used her free hand to buckle her seat belt. "What's up?"

"We've got an emergency," the woman said, without even bothering to return the greeting. "I just hung up with Santa Claus. He called to say he's stuck in traffic in LA and he's not going to be able to get here in time."

Miranda knew the director was referring to the man she had hired to play Santa for the kids at the shelter. Thinking of the children's disappointment, she felt her heart sink.

The words came out before she could stop them. "But the kids are expecting to see Santa Claus."

"I know. I know," the director answered. "The toys are here, but they're going to feel really let down that Santa Claus couldn't make it to hand them out."

Her mind going in all directions, Miranda searched for a solution. And then she thought of something. "Do you still have that old Santa suit from last year?"

"I think so," Amelia answered. "The last time I saw it, it was in the storage room, shoved behind some cans of paint. Why?"

"Find it," she told her. "I'll be at the shelter as soon as I can get there," Miranda promised, terminating the call.

So much for waylaying Colin today, she thought, dropping her phone into her purse.

"Looks like you've gotten a reprieve, Officer Kirby," Miranda murmured under her breath, starting up her vehicle and then peeling out of the hospital's parking lot.

She was going to need padding. Lots and lots of padding if she had a prayer of pulling this off. She'd have to have Amelia round up a whole bunch of pillows.

Miranda was still trying to figure out exactly what she would do as she pulled into the women's shelter's parking lot. If she hadn't been so lost in thought, she would have seen him.

As it was, she didn't.

Not until after she'd jumped out of her car and run smack-dab into him, so hard she all but fell backward. Only Colin grabbing her by the arm kept her from meeting the concrete skull-first.

Stunned, for a split second Miranda thought she was hallucinating—until her brain assured her that she really wasn't conjuring Colin up.

He felt much too real for that.

"Colin?" she cried, shaken. "What are you doing here?" Miranda still wasn't a hundred percent sure that she wasn't just imagining him, putting his face on another man's body.

The police officer released her slowly, watching her intently to make sure she was all right.

"I guess I'm not as noble as I thought," he answered with a self-depreciating shrug.

Maybe she *had* hit her head, Miranda thought,

blinking. She didn't understand what he was telling her. "Why?"

"Because," he confessed, "I was going to stay away from you."

Miranda continued staring at him. He still wasn't making any sense to her.

"Why is staying away 'noble'?" she asked.

He might have known she'd want an explanation. This wasn't easy for him to say. "Because I would only bring you down, and you don't need that."

Miranda thought of the kids in the shelter. She was still in a hurry, but the emergency would have to wait, at least for a couple minutes. This needed to be cleared up, and it needed to be cleared up *now*.

"First of all," she told him, "I do have free will and a mind of my own. I'm not just some ink blotter that indiscriminately absorbs whatever happens to be spilled on it—"

"I'm not saying that you're an ink blotter!" Colin protested.

"I'm not finished," she informed him crisply. "And second of all, I can make up my own mind whom I want or don't want in my life. That's only up to you if you don't want to be in my life because you can't abide being around me."

Colin stared at her in astonishment. How could she even *think* that, much less *say* it?

"You know that's not the case." Angry at how the situation was devolving, he had to rein himself in to keep from shouting the words at Miranda.

"Well, then there's no problem, is there?" she concluded. Turning on her heel, she started to walk toward the building.

Before he could think better of it, Colin caught her by the arm to keep her from leaving. "Oh, there's a problem, all right."

Her desire to resolve this warred with her sense of responsibility. She was going to be cutting it very close, Miranda thought. For all she knew, Amelia might not have located the Santa suit yet.

"Walk with me," she requested. When Colin fell into step beside her, she asked him to elaborate on what he'd just said. "Do you want to tell me just what *is* the problem?"

Colin tried to smother his frustration. He felt as if he was talking to a moving target, but then, that was part and parcel of who this unique creature was.

He thought of waving away her question, or just telling her flatly, "no." But he had started this and had to be man enough to own up to it.

Colin forced himself to say, "I can't get you out of my head."

Miranda's eyes were shining. She spared him a smile as they came up to the shelter's double doors. "Still not seeing the problem."

"But you will," Colin predicted.

She highly doubted that. "Then we'll put a pin in this now and talk about it later. Right now, I have an emergency to deal with," she told him as she reached for the door's brass handle.

So she wasn't just running from him, Colin thought.

Taking charge, he nudged her hand away and opened the door for her. "What sort of an emergency?"

She glanced at her watch. "The Christmas party starts in less than half an hour and Santa Claus is still in LA, stuck in traffic."

Okay, this was convoluted, even for her. "You want to run that by me again? And this time, try to speak slower than the speed of light."

Miranda took a breath. "Amelia hired this professional Santa Claus for the party, and now he can't get here in time because he's stuck in traffic. These kids have been disappointed an awful lot in their lives. I'll be damned if I'm going to let it happen again if I can do something about it."

"Just what is it you have in mind?"

"Amelia said there's an old Santa suit here at the shelter. If we can find it, I'm going to play Santa Claus."

Colin looked at her for a long moment. And then he laughed. Hard. It occurred to Miranda that she had never heard him laugh out loud like that before, but now wasn't the time she wanted to hear it. "You got a better idea?"

It took him a second to collect himself and stop laughing. "Sorry, Miranda, I don't mean to laugh at you, but you just don't look like *anyone's* idea of Santa Claus." He paused again, thinking. And then he nodded. "And yes, I've got a better idea."

She thought she knew what he was going to say and she shook her head, shooting down his idea.

"Just handing out the gifts to the kids isn't going to be enough. These children want Santa Claus giving them those gifts. They want to be normal and see Santa Claus, like every other kid this time of year. They've got a right to that," she insisted passionately.

Just seeing her like this nearly undid Colin. "That wasn't the idea I had," he told her. "Let's go see if we can find that Santa suit. I've got a better chance of pulling this off than you do."

It didn't happen very often, but Miranda found herself practically speechless. When she did recover, she cried, in astonishment, "Really?"

Colin nodded. "Really."

Miranda continued staring at him, waiting for some sort of a punch line. When none came, she had to ask, "You're going to willingly play Santa Claus without having me twist your arm?"

He really did like surprising her.

"Without bending any of my body parts," he assured her. "Now are we going to go on standing here talking about it or are you going to take me to wherever you think that Santa suit is stashed so we can get this show on the road?"

Her response to his question sounded incredibly like a squeal. The next second, Miranda had grabbed his hand and was dragging him through the shelter's main room.

Before they had crossed it, Amelia approached them.

"Did you find it?" Miranda asked breathlessly. "The Santa suit?"

"It's in my office." The director seemed a little surprised by the man Miranda had in tow. "Officer Kirby, it's so nice to see you again. Are you going to be joining the party?"

Before he could answer, Miranda cried, "Definitely!"

Turning on her short, stacked heel, Amelia followed Miranda and the policeman to her office.

Still somewhat bewildered, the woman sounded uncertain as she asked Colin, "You're not going to be playing Santa Claus for the children, are you, Officer Kirby?"

Glancing her way, Miranda answered the question for him. "It's a real Christmas miracle, isn't it?"

The dignified director was smiling so hard she was practically beaming. "It most certainly is. The suit's going to be a little big on you," she warned Colin. "So I found some pillows." She gestured to some stacked on the battered, secondhand easy chair that stood in the corner of her small office.

Colin briefly glanced at them. "They'll work," he told her.

Looking pleased, Amelia said, "Well, I'll give you some privacy…" And she eased herself out of her office.

"And I'll go get the sack of toys ready so you can hand them out," Miranda volunteered. "I'll meet you back here in Amelia's office. If you finish dressing before I return, wait for me. You don't want to go into the main hall empty-handed."

No matter how much Miranda had built up the importance of Santa Claus making an appearance, he knew that the toys were the main attraction. "Not a chance," he assured her.

But as he turned to look at her, he found that he was talking to himself. Miranda had already hurried off.

"That woman's got way too much energy," he murmured as he began to change.

Chapter Sixteen

Miranda turned around when she heard the office door behind her opening. About to tell Colin that she'd gotten the bulging sack of toys for him to hand out while he'd been changing into his costume, she instead wound up saying, "Wow."

"Does it fit all right?" He glanced down at himself critically.

"You look just like Santa Claus," Miranda declared. "I wouldn't have known it was you if I hadn't handed you the costume." She circled him, then nodded with approval. "Laugh."

He eyed her warily. "What?"

"Santa's jolly, remember? You're going to have to go 'ho, ho, ho' at least a few times, so let's hear it."

"Ho, ho, ho," Colin said.

"You're frowning under that beard, aren't you?" she

guessed. "Never mind," she told him when he started to answer. "The beard covers it. But put some gusto into it. And here's your bag of presents." She indicated the sack next to her.

Taking hold of it, he began to swing it over his shoulder. Then his eyes widened. "You carried this here?"

"Dragged, actually," she admitted. "It's kind of heavy."

"That's an understatement," Colin muttered under his breath. "Okay, let's get this over with."

"A little more 'ho, ho, ho' spirit," she advised.

"I'm saving myself," he responded, following her back to the main room.

"Hey, look, everybody! Look who's here," Miranda called out to the children the moment Colin walked into the common area.

The space was filled with kids of all sizes who had been anxiously waiting for the legendary elf to make his appearance. As they turned almost in unison in his direction, their faces lit up with delight, Colin saw.

"It's Santa!"

"Santa's here!"

"Santa!"

A chorus of excited voices called out, creating a cacophony of eagerness and joy blended with disbelief that Santa had actually come to the shelter—and he'd made it ahead of Christmas Eve, as well.

The next second, Colin found himself surrounded as children eagerly rushed up to him.

Miranda took control. Raising her voice, she told the children, "Okay, give him a little space. We don't want to overwhelm Santa. He's still got a lot of places to visit before the holidays are here." Waving the little ones over to her side, she instructed, "Line up, kids. You'll all get your turn, I promise."

As Colin watched in surprise, the children obediently lined up as ordered and patiently awaited their turn.

His eyes shifted in Miranda's direction. This was definitely a new side to her, he thought in admiration.

"That's your cue to get started," she prompted.

"Oh, right." Colin set down his sack and opened it.

To his relief, Miranda stayed by his side the entire time and helped him hand out the gifts. As each child came up to him, she very subtly fed him his or her name to personalize the experience for the child.

Any doubts or uncertainty he'd harbored about volunteering to play Santa vanished within the first few minutes. The excitement, gratitude and awe he saw shining in the eyes of the children who surrounded him managed to create nothing short of an epiphany for Colin.

He began to understand why Miranda did what she did. Being there for these children brought about an incredibly warm feeling that he'd been unacquainted with prior to today.

He really got into the part.

Colin continued digging into the sack and handing out gifts until the very last child in line cried, "Thank you, Santa!" and hurried away, clutching her present against her.

It took him a second to process the fact that there

was no one left in line. Turning toward Miranda, he asked, "Is that it?"

"Yup. You saw every last kid in the place," she told him happily.

The sack sagged as he released it, and it fell to the floor. "Good, because there's only a couple of gifts left. I would have hated to run out of presents before you ran out of kids," he told her. He saw the wide grin on her face. "What?"

"Look at you," she said proudly. "All full of Christmas spirit."

He didn't want her making a big deal of it. "There's a difference between being full of Christmas spirit and not behaving like Scrooge."

"Not in my book," Miranda responded. Leaning into him, she whispered, "Lighten up, Santa, and take the compliment."

Colin glanced down at the suit he was wearing. She saw the look in his eyes and took an educated guess as to what he was thinking. "Itchy, huh?"

He lowered his voice. "You have no idea."

"You held up your end very well," she told him. "Let's get you back to Amelia's office so you can get out of that suit." Miranda looked around at the children, all of whom were happily playing with their toys from Santa. Some were still regarding their gifts in awe. "C'mon, the coast is clear," she whispered. "Let's go."

Following her lead, Colin slipped out of the room. When he didn't hear any of the children calling after him, he breathed a sigh of relief and quickly went down the hall to the small office at the rear of the building.

He went in and was surprised when Miranda followed.

"I'll leave in a minute," she promised, "so you can get out of that costume. I just wanted to indulge a fantasy."

"A fantasy?" he questioned, surprised. She struck him as being so squeaky clean, so grounded, and not the type to have fantasies. His curiosity was aroused. "What kind of a fantasy?"

Mischief danced in her eyes. "I've always wanted to know what it was like to kiss Santa Claus," she told him. "Do you mind?"

Was she kidding? He could feel the whiskers in his fake beard spreading as he grinned. "Not at all."

Miranda wasn't certain just what had possessed her to behave like this. Maybe it was the fact that Colin had volunteered—of his own accord—to help, and by doing so, had literally managed to save the day, which in turn had created a really warm feeling within her.

Or maybe it was because the memory of that last kiss was still lingering on her mind, making her long for a replay. Besides, there was something safe about kissing "Santa Claus" here in the director's office, with a building full of people nearby.

Whatever excuse she gave herself didn't really matter. What did matter was that a moment after she'd asked, she found herself being kissed by "Santa."

Or more specifically, by Colin.

And she discovered that the third time around was even better.

This time, her knees turned to mush right along with the rest of her, and she really did have to hold on for dear life as Colin/Santa deepened the kiss by soul-melting degrees until her mind slipped into a black hole.

Only the sudden awkward noise in the doorway kept the kiss from totally engulfing not just her but both of them.

"Oh, I'm sorry, I—I didn't mean to interrupt," Amelia stuttered, obviously embarrassed about having walked in on them like this. Averting her eyes and addressing the nearby wall, she said, "I just wanted to thank you, Officer Kirby. You really made all those kids extremely happy."

The director turned her head slowly, as if to make sure it was safe to look at them. She breathed a sigh of relief to see that neither was annoyed with her for the accidental intrusion.

"Well, I've said my piece," she added, "so I'll leave you two alone. Thank you again, Officer Kirby."

"Um, yeah. Don't mention it. I got a kick out of it," Colin confessed.

"I'll wait for you out here," Miranda told him, quickly slipping out of the room right behind Amelia. She closed the door in her wake.

When he came out less than five minutes later, the director was nowhere in sight. However, true to her word, Miranda was standing out in the hall close by, waiting for him.

"I'm leaving the suit on the chair in the office," Colin said, nodding toward the room.

"That's perfect," Miranda assured him. "Amelia'll put it away until next year."

He'd already forgotten about the costume. His mind

was on something more important. He searched for the right words.

"Are you going home?" he asked.

Miranda nodded. "Lola's waiting for her dinner. She's probably right in front of the door."

"So she's still with you." It wasn't really a question. He'd just assumed that the dog had become more or less of a fixture at Miranda's house, even though she'd called the situation temporary.

Miranda smiled as she nodded. "Still with me. And I have to say that I'm really getting used to having her around."

"Then why not keep her?"

"It wouldn't be fair," she told him. "Lola needs kids to play with."

He didn't understand why she thought that. "What that dog needs more is love, and you seem to have that covered."

His comment surprised her. It wasn't like him. "I think that Santa suit transformed you."

Colin waved away her assessment. "I don't know what you're talking about. I just say it like it is. Speaking of which…" He let his voice trail off as he framed his next sentence. He didn't want her getting the wrong idea, but didn't want to be so low-key that she turned him down.

When he paused, Miranda cocked her head, waiting for him to finish. "Yes?"

"Would you mind if I came home with you? Just for a while," he qualified a little too quickly. "I feel like I need to wind down a bit after this whole Santa thing."

She laughed. "Too much adulation to handle?" she guessed, amused. This had to be all new to him.

He shrugged carelessly. "Something like that. Is it all right?" he asked, still waiting for her to tell him whether or not he could come over.

"Sure," Miranda replied, wondering why Colin would think that it wouldn't be. "Lola would love to see you."

He laughed drily. Miranda made it sound as if he had some sort of a relationship with the German shepherd. "I'm not so sure about that."

"I am," she said, hooking her arm through his. Thinking he might like to leave with a minimum of fuss, she suggested, "We can take the side door if you want to avoid walking through the main room and running into the kids."

"No, that's all right," he told her. "We can go out the front."

He really had changed, she marveled. And she definitely liked this new, improved Colin. "Maybe you should have put on that Santa suit earlier."

He shrugged. It wasn't the suit; it was what had prompted him to put it on: Miranda.

"Maybe I should have," he allowed casually. "By the way, how was it?"

He'd lost her. "How was what?"

"Back in the director's office, you said you wanted to see what it felt like, kissing Santa Claus," he reminded her. He knew he was leaving himself wide-open, but he was curious about what Miranda would say. "So how was it?"

She smiled up at him and said, "Magical."

He had no idea if she was kidding or not, but they had just entered the common room. Most of the kids were still there and he didn't want to say anything that could draw attention to them, so made no comment on her response.

As they crossed the floor to the front door, he saw the director looking their way. Colin nodded at the woman and she mouthed, *"Thank you."* He smiled in response but kept walking.

"I've got a question for you," Miranda said once they were out the door and in the parking area.

Colin braced himself. "Go ahead."

It was already cold and the wind had picked up. Miranda pulled her jacket more tightly around herself. "How did it feel to save the day? Or is that something you've pretty much gotten used to, being a police officer and all?"

Colin laughed to himself, shaking his head. She was serious, he realized. "Miranda, I'm a motorcycle cop, remember? I usually ruin people's day, not save it."

"You know, it doesn't have to be that way."

"Oh? And what is it that you suggest?" he asked, humoring her.

"Well, did you ever think about switching departments?" Miranda asked.

Colin grew solemn. "I *was* in a different department when I worked in LA."

"What happened?"

His expression grew grim as he remembered. "My partner got killed. On the job," he added. Confronted with that information, she would surely drop the subject. But he'd obviously forgotten who he was dealing with.

"All right," she said slowly, processing what he'd just told her and extrapolating. "Bedford's got a canine unit. You could ask to be transferred there," she told him. She thought of the way he interacted with Lola. "You'd be really good at it."

"We'll see," Colin answered, just to get her to stop taking about it.

But Miranda was on to the way he operated. "Just something to think about," she told him. For now, she tabled the subject. Pointing to her vehicle, which was farther down the lot, she said, "I'm parked over there. Do you want to follow me home?"

"I do know where you live, Miranda," Colin reminded her.

Miranda's smile widened as she inclined her head. "Then I'll see you there. I'll make dinner," she added.

He didn't want her to feel obligated. "You don't have to—"

"I've got to eat," she told him. "And I've seen you eat, so I know that you do, too." She gave him a knowing look. "You don't have to turn everything into a debate, Colin."

He supposed he was guilty of that—at least part of the time. "You do have a way with words."

She grinned. "As long as you know that, everything'll be fine."

He wasn't sure about that, Colin thought, as he walked over to his car. Ever since he'd met Miranda, he'd been doing things completely out of character.

Getting into his vehicle, he started it up and pulled out of the parking lot.

His simple routine of eat, sleep, work, repeat, had gone completely out the window. Ever since he'd moved back to Bedford, he hadn't socialized, even remotely. But since he'd crossed paths with Miranda, he found himself entertaining strange thoughts. He *wanted* to socialize. How else could he explain what he had done today?

Never in his wildest dreams would he have thought that he'd put on a Santa suit, much less wear it for more than two hours the way he'd done, while handing out toys to a whole bunch of kids. Even letting those kids crawl onto his lap, and not just putting up with having some of them hug him, but actually, deep down in his soul, *liking* it.

It felt as if he'd lost sight of all the rules he'd always adhered to. Not just lost sight of them but willfully abandoned them.

If he wasn't careful, he would never be the same again.

What "if"? he silently jeered. There was no "if" about it. He wasn't the same now—and did he even want to be?

All these years, he'd been sleepwalking, moving like a shadow figure through his own life—and that wasn't living at all, he silently insisted.

For weeks now he'd kept thinking that if he hadn't crossed paths with Miranda, his life wouldn't have been turned upside down. As if that was a bad thing.

But maybe it wasn't. Maybe it—and she—had actually been his salvation.

And maybe, he told himself as he approached Miranda's house, he'd be better off if he just stopped thinking altogether.

Chapter Seventeen

Colin never got a chance to ring Miranda's doorbell. The front door flew open the minute he walked up to it.

Seeing the surprised look on his face, Miranda explained, "Lola heard your car pulling up and she barked to let me know you were here. I looked out the window and saw she was right."

Walking in, Colin paused to pet the German shepherd's head. He didn't really have much of a choice since she was blocking his path into the house.

"She let you know it was me," he repeated incredulously.

Moving around them, Miranda smiled as she closed the door. "She has a different bark when a stranger comes."

"I'm flattered, Lola." In response, the dog jumped up, placing her paws against his chest. He had a feeling he knew what she was after. "I'm sorry, girl, I don't have anything for you this time. I came straight here from the shelter."

"Don't worry," Miranda said. "I'm always prepared." To his surprise, she reached around the dog and slipped something into the front pocket of his jeans. "I'm not getting fresh," she told him. "I'm just giving you a couple of treats to give her. What?" she asked, when she saw the amused expression on his face.

"I don't think I've ever heard that phrase—getting fresh—outside of an old movie from the sixties, maybe earlier. No offense," he added quickly. "I think it's kind of cute."

"None taken—now that you've redeemed yourself," she added cheerfully. "C'mon, dinner's on the table."

Colin stared at the back of her head, stunned, as he followed her to the dining room. "How did you manage to get anything ready so fast? You couldn't have gotten here more than five minutes ago."

"Ten," she corrected. "I know a shortcut. And I really didn't have to cook. Those are leftovers from yesterday." She gestured at the covered tureen in the center of the table. "Nothing fancy. Just some chicken Alfredo over angel-hair spaghetti."

"Leftovers," Colin repeated, nodding. "That makes more sense. I didn't think even you were *that* fast."

She dished out the spaghetti, then the chicken Alfredo, first on one plate, then the other.

"Am I being challenged?" she asked him, the corners of her mouth curving.

"I didn't mean it that way," he said, then qualified, "Unless you wanted me to."

All she wanted right now was to sit down to a peaceful dinner with him.

"Eat," she prompted. "Dinner's getting cold. And, you," she said, looking down at Lola, who had presented herself at the table. "Let the man eat in peace, girl. He already gave you a bribe."

He was amused by the dog's antics. "I think she's expecting more."

Miranda sighed. "You were right. I have been spoiling her. But her new owner is going to do a better job of making her toe the line," she said.

Surprised, Colin lowered his fork. "New owner? Lola's been adopted?"

Miranda nodded, looking oddly calm to him. He would have expected her to be more upset. "Her papers were all put through and her fee was paid."

"Fee?" he questioned. He had no idea how pet adoption was conducted.

"Every dog and cat that the shelter takes in gets all their shots and they're neutered or spayed, depending on the animal's gender. When they're adopted, the new owner is charged a nominal fee for those services. It's to ensure that the next homeless animal can be taken care of."

Something didn't make sense to him. "If Lola's been adopted, why is she still here?" he asked.

The surge of disappointment he was experiencing over the news of the adoption really caught him off guard. He realized with a pang that he was going to miss Lola once her owner picked her up.

"That's rather a funny story," Miranda answered. "I'll tell it to you once we finish eating."

Colin filled in the blanks: they were going to be taking Lola to her new owner right after dinner. That was why Miranda was holding off telling him the story until later.

He honestly didn't know if he wanted to go with her. Watching the German shepherd being handed over to someone else wasn't something he wanted to witness.

But then it occurred to him that maybe Miranda was asking him to come along because *she* was going to need some moral support for this. He knew that she had gotten close to the animal. She'd said as much herself. What surprised him was that he had, too.

Picking up his fork again, Colin continued to eat, but he was no longer tasting anything and twice had to rouse himself because he'd missed what Miranda was saying.

"You're awfully quiet," she noted, finishing her dinner.

"I'm just thinking," Colin told her without elaborating.

"Okay," she announced, rising from the table. "Let's do this."

He looked at the empty plates on the table. She was leaving them where they were. "You're not going to do the dishes first?"

"They can wait," she told him loftily. "I'll do them later."

That wasn't like her. Giving up Lola and taking her to her new owner was undoubtedly hard on Miranda, he thought. He wanted to shield her from this, but had no idea how.

"Okay, let's get it over with," he told her.

Responding, Miranda took his hand and led him into the living room.

"Aren't you forgetting something?" he asked, nodding at Lola. Miranda hadn't stopped to put a leash on the dog. In fact, she'd left her in the dining room, gnawing on a bone that she had given her.

"I don't think so," Miranda answered innocently.

Instead of walking to the front door, she stopped in front of the Christmas tree. Bending down, she picked up a flat, rectangular box sporting shiny blue wrapping paper and held it out to him.

"Merry Christmas," Miranda declared. "A little early."

"What is it?" he asked, perplexed.

When he didn't take it from her, she gently shoved the box into his hands. "You could open it and see."

She was being very mysterious about this, Colin thought. Still not opening it, he told her uncomfortably, "I didn't get you anything."

"You've given me more than you think—and you were Santa Claus for all those kids," she added. "Now, are you going to open that? Or are you going to just keep looking at it?"

He would have preferred going with the latter, but knew that wouldn't be fair to her, especially after she had gone through all the trouble of not just getting him something but wrapping it, as well.

Colin made his decision. "I'll open it."

"Good choice," she told him with approval. Watching him do so, she could only marvel. "You tear off wrapping paper slower than anyone I've ever seen." Finally, he finished removing the wrapping paper to reveal a decorative gift box beneath. "Now take the top off the box and see what's in it," she coaxed.

When he did, Colin found paperwork. Specifically, paperwork that belonged to Lola, saying that she'd received her rabies vaccination as well as a number of other vaccinations. There was also confirmation of a license registration with the city of Bedford that was good for one year. The certificate stated that her name was Lola Kirby and that she belonged to—

Colin's head jerked up. "Me?" he asked, stunned. "I'm Lola's owner?"

Nodding, Miranda told him, "I didn't know what to get you for Christmas and then it came to me. You needed to have a friendly face to come home to, and Lola needed a home. It seemed like the perfect solution."

"But I can't take care of her," he protested. "I'm never home."

"Sure, you can take care of her. And when you need to take a break, you can leave her with me. I'll dog-sit Lola for you," she volunteered cheerfully.

He was as close to being speechless as he had ever been in his life. Shaking his head, Colin muttered, "I don't know what to say—you're crazy, you know that?"

"I would have accepted 'Thank you, Miranda. It's just what I wanted,'" she responded. Then, growing serious, she told him, "I saw it in your eyes, you know. The way you felt about Lola."

Moved, he came closer to her. So close there was hardly any space for even a breath between them. His gaze met hers. "What else did you see in my eyes?"

Lola was still in the dining room, working away at her soup bone. Except for the sound of teeth meeting bone, there was nothing but silence in the house.

Silence and heat.

"What else was I supposed to see in your eyes?" Miranda asked, her voice dropping to barely a whisper. Her mouth suddenly felt extremely dry, even as she felt her pulse accelerating, going double time.

"You, Miranda," he replied softly. "You were supposed to see you."

She could hardly breathe. "I thought that was just wishful thinking on my part," she confessed.

"You're trembling," he said.

She couldn't seem to stop. Grasping at straws, she said the first thing that came to mind. "It's cold in here."

"Then I guess I'll have to warm you up," Colin told her, his voice low and seductive as he took her into his arms.

The next thing she knew, Colin had lowered his mouth to hers.

And then the whole world slipped into an inky, endless abyss. There was nothing left except the two of them.

This time, there was no hesitation, no second thoughts.

For the first time since he'd met her, he felt no need to put on the brakes, or to tell himself that being with her like this was a mistake.

He wanted her.

Wanted her more than he wanted to breathe.

Because he had come to understand that this woman was what made his existence worthwhile. Just by being herself, she had brought happiness into his life. She'd taken his dark existence and illuminated it, bringing color into his world.

Color and warmth and desire in such proportions they completely overwhelmed him.

And humbled him.

He kissed Miranda over and over again, each kiss more soul-stirring than the one that had come before it. And then, just as she was about to utterly succumb to the passion that was making her head spin, he drew back for a moment.

Miranda felt confusion taking hold.

Oh Lord, he wasn't stopping again, was he? She didn't think she could bear it if he stopped.

Colin drew in a shaky breath. He needed to make his intention clear to her. He didn't want Miranda to look back on this later and feel that he had somehow used the madness of the moment to take advantage of her.

He wanted to be sure—and most of all, he wanted *her* to be sure.

"Miranda, I want to make love with you."

A laugh escaped her lips, a laugh of relief. "It's about time."

And then suddenly, just like that, everything felt right.

He kissed her with more eagerness than he thought he could possibly possess. His lips never left hers as desire surged through him, guiding him.

Controlling him.

He didn't remember undressing her, but he remembered every smooth, tempting curve of her body once her clothing had been stripped away. Remembered the thrill of passing his hands slowly over her silky skin. Remembered the rush he felt as he mentally cataloged every part of her, making it his.

Passion grew to incredible proportions, demanding an appeasement that couldn't be reached, because each time he drew closer to the peak, it moved that much further out of reach, tempting him to kept going, to keep taking refuge in all parts of her, in everything she had to offer.

The sound of her breathing, growing shorter and more audible, drove him wild.

He wanted to take her now, this moment. Wanted to bury himself in her. But with iron control, he reined himself in.

For her.

He wanted Miranda to remember this night, to remember him, and for that to happen, he needed to slow down. To make this all about her—and that, in turn, would make it about them, which had become so very important to him.

Sweeping her up in his arms, he carried her to her bedroom. He closed the door with his back, automatically creating their own private little world. Carrying her over to her bed, Colin placed her down on it gently.

His heart was hammering in his chest and echoing in his head as he lay down beside her. Demands collided within him, making it increasingly difficult to hold himself in check, to not give in to the ever-mounting desire just to take her.

Somehow, he managed to pace himself, but it was the hardest thing he had ever done.

Trailing his lips along Miranda's body, he anointed every part of her, thrilling to the sight and to the feel of her growing more and more excited. She was twisting and turning beneath him as if trying to absorb every sensation that he was creating for her.

With her.

When she ran her hands up and down his torso, when she turned the tables and mirrored all his movements, spiking his desire to unbelievable heights, Colin came exceedingly close to losing total control. But again, at the last moment, he caught himself, vowing to go one more round before he surrendered and made them into one joined being.

He feasted on her lips, the hollow of her throat, working his way down to her belly and farther. Her unbridled gasp when he brought her to her first climax reverberated within his chest, exciting him so much that he tottered on the very edge of restraint.

And then, fearing he couldn't hold on for even another heartbeat, Colin worked his way back up along her damp body, with Miranda rising and twisting against him as he went.

Suddenly, he was over her, his eyes meeting hers, his fingers entwining with hers.

Her legs parted beneath him, issuing a silent invitation he welcomed with every fiber of his aching being. When he entered her, they instantly moved together as if this was the way it was always meant to be. The tempo increased, the rhythm grew to demanding proportions that neither of them was capable of resisting.

Passion wrapped heated wings around them as they raced to the very top of the summit. To the very end of their journey.

When the explosion finally came, fireworks of majestic dimensions showered over them.

And Colin clung to her as if she was his very salvation.

Because she was.

Chapter Eighteen

A myriad of feelings vied for space within Colin as the heated, comforting glow of euphoria he'd been experiencing slowly began to recede. Feelings he wasn't able to completely sort out just yet.

Feelings that had been missing from his life for more than a decade.

As fierce passions settled down, he drew Miranda to him, happy just to have her here next to him on the bed. Contentment, something he was unfamiliar with up until now, washed over him.

He felt like a different person.

Colin wondered if there was a way he could remain here like this indefinitely, her breath mingling with his, the scent of the light, flowery body wash she used filling his senses.

He came close to drifting off when a noise caught his attention.

Moving his head to hear better, Colin couldn't quite place the sound. "You hear something?" he asked Miranda.

She turned her face toward him, managing to rub her cheek against his chest. He could literally feel her smile on his skin.

Raising her head just a little, she looked at him. "You can't tell what that is?"

"So then you *do* hear something." He was beginning to think that he was imagining it.

"Sure. That's Lola scratching against the door," she murmured. "I guess she finished gnawing on that bone and decided to track you down."

"Me?" he questioned. "Why me?" It didn't make any sense to him.

"My guess is that she wants your attention." He could feel heat beginning to travel through his body again as every inch of Miranda seemed to be smiling at him. "Why don't you open the door and let her in?"

"In here?" he asked, surprised.

Miranda didn't see why he would hesitate. "Why not? She's got the run of the place already."

"But we just, um…" Colin seemed to trip over his tongue.

She hadn't thought that he could be this incredibly sweet, so delicate that he didn't know how to go about saying that they'd just made love. She came to his rescue and glossed right over his meaning.

"Which is why she probably tracked you down," Miranda told him. "Lola knows that you're the alpha male and she wants to be the alpha female."

Colin stared at the woman in his arms, stunned as well as confused. "This is getting way out of hand. I don't understand any of it."

Miranda laughed. "Don't worry," she said, patting his chest. "I'm here to talk you through this if you need help. Just think of Lola as a fuzzy child. She needs discipline, a firm hand and lots of love—just like any child."

Colin sat up, looking at the door. The scratching continued.

He dragged a hand through his hair, trying to think, and feeling totally out of his element. "Taking care of a dog is a lot of responsibility."

"Yes, but it has a lot of compensation, too. Like boundless love."

He still looked uncertain. "I don't think I'm ready for this."

Since he wasn't getting up, Miranda did, wrapping the sheet around her.

"Not ready for being on the receiving end of boundless love? Sure you are," she exclaimed, making it sound as if she knew him better than he knew himself.

But he was thinking of the responsibility part. "No, if I'm going to be her new owner, I'm definitely going to need help," he said, looking at Miranda pointedly.

Meanwhile, she had opened the door and Lola came flying in. In two steps the German shepherd went from standing out in the hallway to standing on the bed. She came close to knocking Colin off the mattress in her enthusiasm and then started licking his face.

"Lots and lots of help," Colin declared, doing his best to sit up again and gain some semblance of the upper hand over the dog.

Miranda laughed as, still wearing the sheet like a Roman toga, she climbed back into bed. Lola was between them and was acting as if this was some sort of new game. Her head practically spun as she looked from one of them to the other, as if to say that she didn't know the rules to this game yet, but was more than willing to play.

Watching her, Miranda stated, "I think she wants you to pet her."

Stroking the animal, he looked over Lola's head at Miranda. "Now you see, I'm going to need that sort of insight to help me navigate through this pet ownership thing."

She was certainly on board with that, Miranda thought. "Like I said, you can give me a call anytime you need help."

"I appreciate that," he told her. "But then you'd have to find the time to come over, or I'd have to come over to you and bring the dog. That would consume an awful lot of downtime and we're both pretty busy as it is."

She knew she'd taken a chance when she'd decided to make him Lola's owner, but she'd thought he would last longer than a few hours.

Miranda took a breath, resigning herself to the inevitable. "You're saying you don't want the dog." She gave it one more shot, taking Lola's muzzle in her hands and turning the dog's head in his direction. "How can you say no to this face?"

"I'm not saying no," Colin told her. "I'm saying we need a different solution."

She took the only guess open to her. "You're saying you want her to stay with me."

But Colin shook his head. Stroking the dog's back— Lola had settled down and was now lying in the bed, content to have one of them on either side—he said, "That's not it, either."

At a loss now, she asked, "All right then, so what is it?"

Nerves all but got the better of him. This was brand-new territory for him and he didn't know how she would receive what he was about to say. "If you stop making guesses and just listen, I'll tell you." The moment the words were out of his mouth, he knew he'd sounded short with her.

"Okay." Miranda crossed her arms, waiting for him to go on.

The sheet slipped down just enough to give him a tantalizing glimpse of what he'd availed himself of earlier. Thinking about that, Colin found he had to struggle to keep his mind on what he was trying to say.

"So talk," she prompted, when he remained silent.

Here went nothing, Colin decided.

"I thought that we could move in together," he told her.

He was surprised that the words came out as easily as they did.

Miranda's mouth dropped open. But not a single sound emerged.

She was speechless, he realized, and he didn't know if that was a good thing or a bad one. Was she trying to find the words to turn him down gently, or was she so shocked that she'd lost the ability to talk?

"Move in together," she said, repeating his words.

"Yes," he confirmed, then went on to elaborate. "You could move in with me. But my place is small. It's an apartment and it might be kind of crowded for you, especially with Lola. Or I could move in here," he said, watching Miranda's face intently for her reaction.

"Move in together," she repeated again. "For the sake of the dog." The last words were uttered in semi-disbelief.

"Well, yes," he agreed. Something was off and he felt like a man trying to walk across a lake on very thin ice. He could feel the ice cracking beneath his feet with every step he took, yet he had no choice but to forge on. "You were the one who gave her to me, so I figured you'd want to do what was best for her."

"You want to move in together because of the dog," she said, as if trying to wrap her mind around what he was telling her.

"Well, that's one reason," he agreed. He was having a devil of a time getting the words out.

"Oh, so there's another reason?" she asked innocently.

Feeling awkward and totally inarticulate, not to mention afraid of being turned down once he told her the real reason behind his suggestion, Colin seriously thought about throwing up his hands and just abandoning the whole idea, lock, stock and barrel.

But then something egged him on.

It was all or nothing.

If he didn't say anything, he'd already lost, so there was nothing to lose by speaking up.

Frustrated, he shouted at her, "Of course there's another reason."

Lola instantly sat up, a canine barrier intent on protecting whichever one of them needed protecting.

"It's okay, Lola," Miranda said soothingly, rubbing the tip of the animal's ear, a trick she'd learned to calm a dog down. "It's okay. Lie down, girl."

After a moment, the dog obeyed.

"Okay," Miranda said, turning her attention back to him. "You were saying there was another reason…" She trailed off, waiting for him to pick up the conversation.

"You know there's another reason," he told her. When she continued silently looking at him, waiting, he blew out a breath. "You're going to make me say this, aren't you?"

"I'm afraid so." The corners of her mouth curved ever so slightly. "I need clarification, Colin. What's the other reason you want us to move in together?"

Exasperated, he raised his voice again. "Because I love you, damn it."

She struggled not to laugh. "Is that one word?"

"Miranda…" He sounded very close to the end of his rope.

Once again she came to his rescue. "I love you, too, damn it," Miranda said, mimicking his exact intonation. And then she asked, "Are you sure about this?" She would hate for him to look back with regret because it had all come about in the heat of the moment.

"Sure that I love you?" he questioned. "Yes, I'm sure. I just didn't want to have to say it. Putting myself out there is hard for me," he told her. "It's not something I do."

Reaching over the dog, who appeared to be close to falling asleep, she touched Colin's face and smiled. "I was talking about moving in together, but what you just said was very nice."

"Just 'very nice'?" he asked in surprise, mimicking *her* intonation.

There was humor in Miranda's eyes as she told him honestly, "I'm afraid if I say any more, I'll scare you off."

"After everything I've just been through, that is *not* going to happen," he stated.

"Since words are so difficult for you—" Miranda rose up on her knees, allowing the sheet to fall away and pool around her thighs "—why don't I just show you how I feel about what you said?"

She was about to lean into him when Colin put a finger to her lips, stopping her. "Hold that thought."

The next moment, he got off the bed, coaxing the dog to do the same. Holding on to Lola's collar, he guided the animal to the bedroom's threshold.

"C'mon, girl," he told her, "you need to go back into the other room for a few minutes."

"Just a few minutes?" Miranda pretended to question him.

"Maybe an hour—or two," he amended.

After taking Lola out, Colin was gone for a couple minutes. Returning, he made sure to close the door behind him.

Miranda cocked her head, listening for a moment for scratching noises.

Or whining.

She heard neither.

"Nothing," she said. "You really are good at disciplining." She wove her arms around his neck as he joined her.

Rather than say anything in response to her compliment, Colin murmured, "I hope you didn't have any plans for that other soup bone in the refrigerator."

So that was why the dog was so quiet. Miranda could only laugh. "You're as bad as I am."

"I really hope so," he told her.

And with that, there was no more talk. About anything. He had far better things to do than talk, and was more than eager to get started.

Epilogue

"Ladies, I think that it's pretty safe to say this is quite possibly the most unique wedding venue we have ever attended," Maizie told her two friends as she sat on the white folding chair between Theresa and Celia.

There was row after row of folding chairs in the hospital rec room, in the same area of the children's ward that just a few months ago had housed the giant Christmas tree.

The large room was all but filled to capacity with small patients from the ward, a great many women and children from the shelter, and several volunteers who worked with Miranda at the animal shelter.

"Thank goodness Miranda's mother and Colin's aunt were here early to make sure the altar was set up before it got so crowded in here," Theresa commented.

She and her catering team had arrived early, as well.

Working quickly, they had prepared everything for the reception that was to follow immediately after the ceremony.

"If they knew there was going to be this many people attending, why didn't they just opt for someplace bigger?" Celia asked.

"That's simple enough to answer," Theresa told her. "Miranda didn't want the children here missing the wedding. A lot of them aren't able or well enough to leave the hospital—and all of them are very attached to her. Miranda wouldn't dream of leaving any of them out."

Maizie nodded, pleased. "You ask me, Colin's getting a hell of a girl," she said to her friends. "There aren't many young women who are that thoughtful."

Theresa was beaming as she kept her eyes peeled for any sign that the bride was about to enter. "I really think that we outdid ourselves with this particular match, girls."

"Well, none of this would have happened if Maizie hadn't charmed that desk sergeant into rescheduling Colin's regular route so that he'd be right there when Miranda whizzed by," Celia commented. She turned toward Maizie. "How *did* you know that Miranda would be driving too fast?"

"And how did you really get that sergeant to change Colin's schedule with the other police officer's?" Theresa asked.

Maizie merely smiled, remaining tight-lipped, at least for now. "A girl's got to have some secrets, ladies," she told them with a wink.

"Not at this stage she doesn't," Celia told her life-long friend.

"Shh, they're starting to play the wedding march. You don't want to miss any of this," Maizie said.

Those who could rose to their feet. The rest of the attendees remained seated, anxiously anticipating the entrance of the bride.

Miranda was standing just outside the recreation room's closed doors, holding on to her bouquet of pink and white carnations and willing the sudden burst of butterflies in her stomach to go away.

"Nervous, darling?" Jeannine asked her daughter.

"A little. Mostly just afraid of tripping before I reach the altar," Miranda answered, a small smile curving her lips.

"You won't," Jeannine said confidently. "You're the steadiest person I ever knew."

Miranda took a breath, pressing one hand against her stomach as if that would get the butterflies to settle down.

"I wish your father was here," Jeannine said in a soft whisper. "He would have loved to see you in your bridal gown."

"He's here, Mom. I can feel it." The music swelled. Miranda took a breath. "That's our cue."

"I love you, Miranda," Jeannine told her.

"And I love you." She looked at her mother. The woman's cheeks were wet. "Please don't cry, Mom. You'll get your contacts all foggy."

Jeannine laughed, brushing the tears away. "Don't worry, I'll get you there. I promise."

The doors parted, drawn open by two of the orderlies. Miranda saw a sea of faces turning in her direction, but they all blended together before her eyes. Looking out at them, she could make out only one face in that enormous crowd.

The only face that mattered to her right at this moment.

Colin's face.

He was standing at the altar, looking incredibly handsome in his black tuxedo and dark gray shirt. She had half expected him to come in his police uniform. She wouldn't have cared what he wore, as long as he came.

"Ready, darling?" Jeannine asked.

Her eyes not leaving the man she had never expected to come into her life, Miranda answered, "More than ready, Mom."

They made their way up the makeshift aisle until they reached the minister, who was standing in front of the altar, waiting to say the words that would join her to Colin.

"Who gives this woman?" the man asked when she came before him.

"I do," Jeannine replied, her voice trembling. And then she withdrew so that the ceremony could begin.

"You look beautiful," Colin whispered to Miranda.

"You do, too," she told him.

He nearly laughed. It was a good feeling, he couldn't help thinking. Miranda had brought laughter into his life and into his heart.

More than a few of the children giggled as they

watched Lola trot up the aisle next, the wedding rings tied around her neck with a navy blue bow.

"We can begin," the minister announced.

Colin never thought he would ever be this lucky. When he looked at Miranda, just before they began to exchange their vows and their rings, he realized that she was thinking the same thing.

He could see it in her eyes.

They really were meant for one another, he thought. And he for one would always be eternally grateful for that.

* * * * *

For even more Christmas cheer from
Marie Ferrarella, make sure to check out
A BABY FOR CHRISTMAS
Available now from Harlequin Western Romance!

Don't miss previous titles in the
MATCHMAKING MAMAS *miniseries:*

A SECOND CHANCE FOR THE SINGLE DAD
MEANT TO BE MINE

Available now from Harlequin Special Edition.

And keep an eye out for
AN ENGAGEMENT FOR TWO,
the next book in this heartwarming miniseries,
releasing in February 2018!

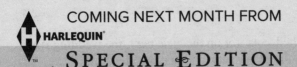
Available December 19, 2017

#2593 HER SOLDIER OF FORTUNE
The Fortunes of Texas: The Rulebreakers • by Michelle Major
When Nathan Fortune returned home, he vowed to put the past behind him. But when Bianca, his best friend's little sister, shows up with her son, Nate finds that the past won't stay buried...and it threatens to snuff out the future Nate and Bianca now hope to build with each other.

#2594 THE ARIZONA LAWMAN
Men of the West • by Stella Bagwell
Tessa Parker goes to Arizona to investigate her unexpected inheritance and gets more than a ranch. There's a sexy deputy next door and perhaps this orphan may finally find a family on the horizon.

#2595 JUST WHAT THE COWBOY NEEDED
The Bachelors of Blackwater Lake • by Teresa Southwick
Logan Hunt needs a nanny. What he gets is pretty kindergarten teacher Grace Flynn, whose desire for roots and a family flies right in the face of Logan's determination to remain a bachelor. Can Logan overcome his fears of becoming his father in time to convince Grace that she's exactly what he wants?

#2596 CLAIMING THE CAPTAIN'S BABY
American Heroes • by Rochelle Alers
Former army captain and current billionaire Giles Wainwright is shocked to learn he has a daughter and even more shocked at how attracted he is to her adoptive mother, Mya Lawson. But Mya doesn't trust Giles's motives when it comes to her heart and he will have to work harder than ever if he wants to claim Mya's love.

#2597 THE RANCHER AND THE CITY GIRL
Sweet Briar Sweethearts • by Kathy Douglass
Running for her life, Camille Parker heads to her sworn enemy, Jericho Jones, for protection. She may be safe from those who wish her harm, but as they both come to see their past presumptions proven incorrect, Camille's heart is more at risk than ever.

#2598 BAYSIDE'S MOST UNEXPECTED BRIDE
Saved by the Blog • by Kerri Carpenter
Riley Hudson is falling for her best friend and boss, Sawyer Wallace, the only person who knows she is the ubiquitous Bayside Blogger. Awkward as that could be, though, they both have bigger problems in the form of blackmail and threats to close down the newspaper they both work for! Will Sawyer see past that long enough to make Riley Bayside's most unexpected bride?

YOU CAN FIND MORE INFORMATION ON UPCOMING HARLEQUIN® TITLES, FREE EXCERPTS AND MORE AT WWW.HARLEQUIN.COM.

HSECNM1217

Get 2 Free Books,
Plus 2 Free Gifts—
just for trying the Reader Service!

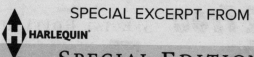
"He's an idiot," Nate offered automatically.

One side of her mouth kicked up. "You sound like
Eddie. He never liked Brett, even when we were first
dating. He said he wasn't good enough for me."

"Obviously that's true." Nate took a step closer
but stopped himself before he reached for her. Bianca
didn't belong to him, and he had no claim on her. But
one morning with EJ and he already felt a connection to
the boy. A connection he also wanted to explore with the
beautiful woman in front of him. "Any man who would
walk away from you needs to have his—" He paused,
feeling the unfamiliar sensation of color rising to his face.
His mother had certainly raised him better than to swear
in front of a lady, yet the thought of Bianca being hurt by
her ex made his blood boil. "He needs a swift kick in the
pants."

"Agreed," she said with a bright smile. A smile that

made him weak in the knees. He wanted to give her a reason to smile like that every day. "I'm better off without him, but it still makes me sad for EJ. I do my best, but it's hard with only the two of us. There are so many things we've had to sacrifice." She wrapped her arms around her waist and turned to gaze out of the barn, as if she couldn't bear to make eye contact with Nate any longer. "Sometimes I wish I could give him more."

"You're enough," he said, reaching out a hand to brush away the lone tear that tracked down her cheek. "Don't doubt for one second that you're enough."

As he'd imagined, her skin felt like velvet under his callused fingertip. Her eyes drifted shut and she tipped up her face, as if she craved his touch as much as he wanted to give it to her.

He wanted more from this woman—this moment—than he'd dreamed possible. A loose strand of hair brushed the back of his hand, sending shivers across his skin.

She glanced at him from beneath her lashes, but there was no hesitation in her gaze. Her liquid brown eyes held only invitation, and his entire world narrowed to the thought of kissing Bianca.

"I finished with the hay, Mommy," EJ called from behind him.

Don't miss
HER SOLDIER OF FORTUNE by Michelle Major,
available January 2018 wherever
Harlequin® Special Edition books and ebooks are sold.

www.Harlequin.com

THE WORLD IS BETTER WITH

Romance

Harlequin has everything from contemporary, passionate and heartwarming to suspenseful and inspirational stories.

Whatever your mood, we have a romance just for you!